99¢ ebook

I0608244

THE GHOST STORY MEGAPACK

25 Classic Tales by Masters

**Mary Elizabeth Braddon • Jerome K. Jerome
Bram Stoker • Rudyard Kipling • Edith Nesbit
E. F. Benson • Wilkie Collins • Mark Twain
H. de Vere Stacpoole • Thomas Hardy • More!**

Buy direct from wildsidepress.com
or search for "megapack" at amazon.com
or any other major ebook site!

Also available
The Science Fiction Megaback
The Horror Megapack,
The Mystery Megapack
The Western Megapack,

Weird Tales ®

FALL 2009

SUBSCRIBE AT **WWW.WEIRDTALESMAGAZINE.COM**

WEIRD TALES was the *first* storytelling magazine devoted explicitly to the realm of the **dark and fantastic.**

Founded in 1923, WEIRD TALES provided a literary home for such diverse wielders of the imagination as **H.P. Lovecraft** (creator of Cthulhu), **Robert E. Howard** (creator of Conan the Barbarian), **Margaret Brundage** (artistic godmother of goth fetishism), and **Ray Bradbury** (author of *The Illustrated Man* and *Something Wicked This Way Comes*).

Today, O wondrous reader of the 21st century, we continue to seek out that which is most weird and unsettling, for your own edification

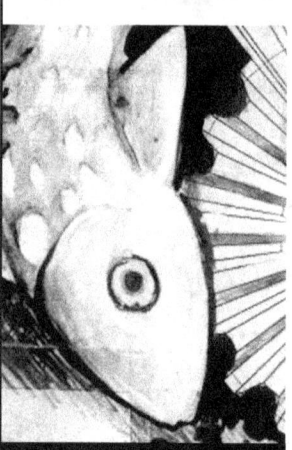

FICTION

POETRY

EDITORIAL & CREATIVE DIRECTOR Stephen H. Segal FICTION EDITOR Ann VanderMeer
CONTRIBUTING EDITORS Amanda Gannon, Kenneth Hite, Darrell Schweitzer
ASSISTANT EDITOR/ONLINE Vanessa Ellis ASSISTANT EDITOR/OUTREACH Rae Bryant
EDITORIAL ASSISTANTS Chelsea Bauch, Tessa Kum CONTRIBUTING ARTISTS Steven Archer,
Molly Crabapple, Alex Eckman-Lawn, Ira Marcks, Marc Robinson

PUBLISHER John Gregory Betancourt EDITOR EMERITUS George H. Scithers

*All writers
of such stories
are prophets*

SPECIAL FEATURE
Happy 200th Birthday, Edgar Allan Poe

DEPARTMENTS

COVER ILLUSTRATION | **"Thaumaturge" by Andrew Trabbold**

ANDREWTRABBOLD.BLOGSPOT.COM • TRABBOLD.DEVIANTART.COM

VOL. 64, NO. 2 | **Issue 354**

WEIRD TALES ® is published by Wildside
Press, LLC. Postmaster and others: send
all changes of address and other sub-
scription matters to Wildside Press, 9710
Traville Gateway Dr. #234, Rockville MD
20850–7408. Single copies, $6.99 in U.S.A.
& possessions; $10 by first class mail
elsewhere. Subscriptions: 4 issues $20
in U.S.A. & possessions; $40 elsewhere,
in U.S. funds. Single-copy orders should
be addressed to WEIRD TALES at the
address above. Copyright © 2009 by
Wildside Press, LLC. All rights reserved;
reproduction prohibited without prior
permission. Typeset & printed in the
United States of America. WEIRD TALES
® is a registered trademark owned by
Weird Tales, Limited.

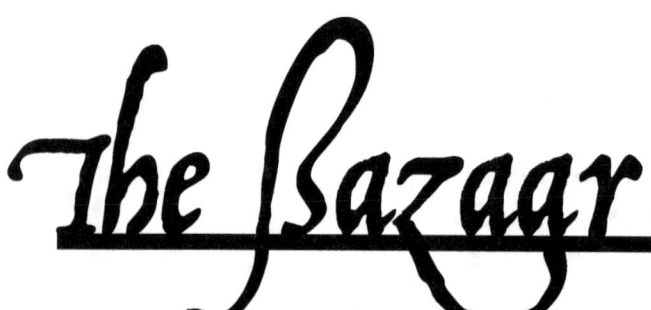

The Bazaar

STRANGE ARTISANS & ARTIFACTS

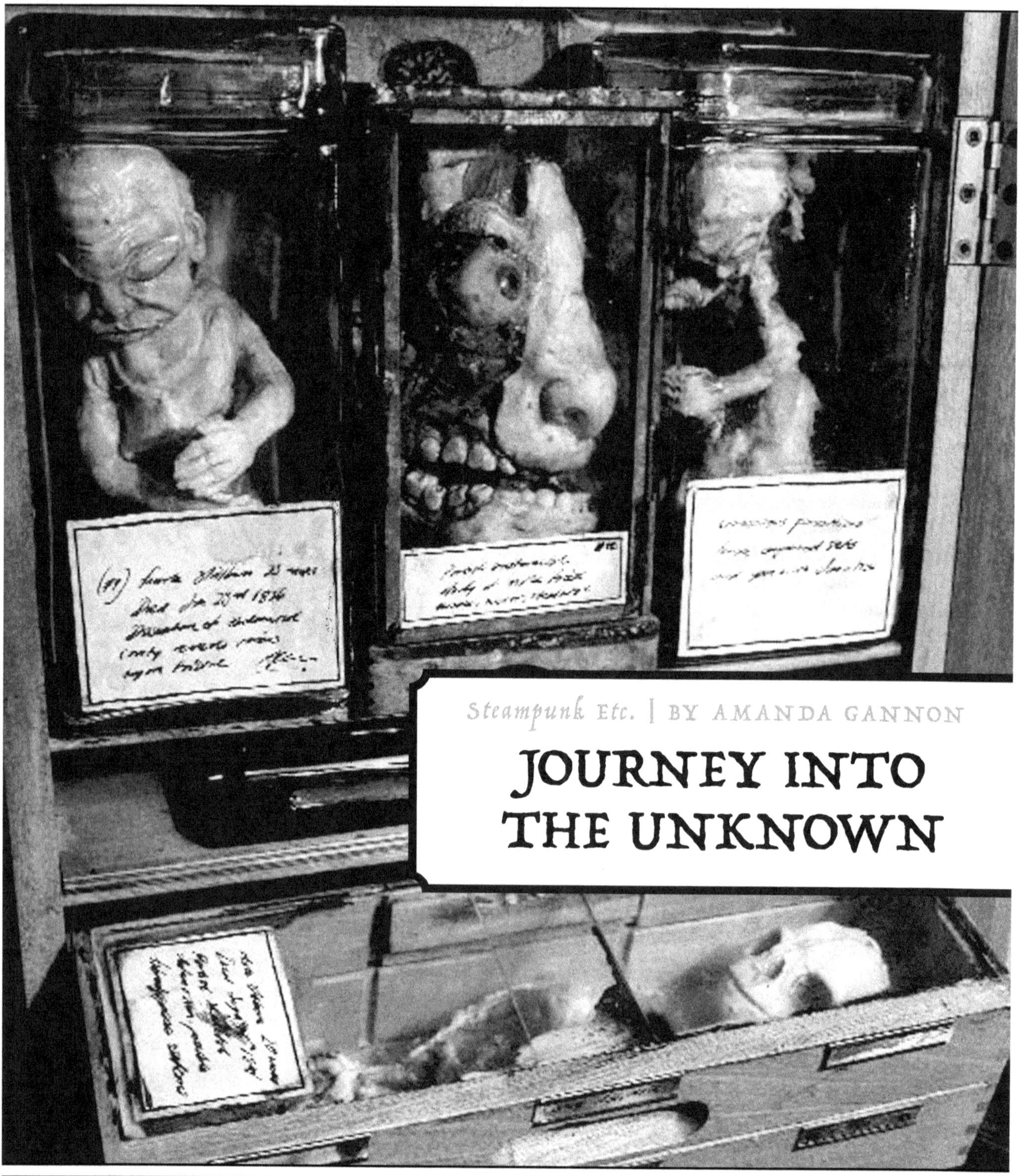

Steampunk Etc. | BY AMANDA GANNON

JOURNEY INTO THE UNKNOWN

What treasures lie within Alex CF's expedition cases?

THE LOCK HAS been chipped away, and the battered old case swings open easily to reveal a biologist's field kit, complete with a selection of dissecting tools, rows of test tubes, and bottles full of samples: tissue, hair, teeth. Then we find a crucifix—a jarring, superstitious note that adds to our growing unease. And finally there is a jar, well-sealed and very old. Tucked next to it, a diary and several pages of hastily-scribbled notes testify to the reality of what lies within. It's a cryptozoologist's dearest dream, or worst nightmare: a complete werewolf fetus. Everything falls into place, realizations like clockwork.

Faced with such tangible evidence right in our hands, it's overwhelmingly tempting to *believe*—yet werewolves are figments of our imagination and lycanthropy has been scientifically explained away. Where, then, did this case of mysteries come from?

Meet Alex CF, a U.K.-based "cryptozoological pseudo-scientific assemblage artist and illustrator" who specializes in creating relics of a nonexistent past. He brings each such project to life, like the lycanthrope research case, in meticulous detail. The process can take weeks as Alex gathers materials, sculpts creatures, assembles machines, creates slides, fills journals with notes and drawings, and replicates vintage photographs and daguerreotypes.

The appearance of *age* is the critical fiction here, the factor without which suspension of disbelief cannot occur. Alex's techniques yield completely convincing results; real antiques lie side by side with artifacts the artist has created from modern materials, and—save for those items we *know* cannot exist—the two are indistinguishable from one another.

Exploring these artifacts fosters a quiet, subtle horror, and also an illicit thrill—a sensation familiar to anyone who has ever spent hours poking through attics, libraries, and strange old museums hoping for a glimpse of the unknown. Alex's art represents forbidden knowledge, indeed: stories of humanity's inhuman past, prehistoric plateaus, failed experiments, and vanishing species that never were.

Alex lavishes particular attention upon his creatures. The albino werewolf fetus seems asleep in a hand-labeled jar of preservative, hairs stirring. The dessicated body of an infant triceratops lies on a bed of excelsior, all sunken, pebbled skin and bony ridges. They are absolutely believable as real creatures, primitively preserved.

Alex's work provides a glimpse into a time that never was, a world where the borders between science and the unknown are far wider than they are here snf now. It's a world of time travel and werewolves, vampire hunters, Elder Things, and frightening truths; a world in which Doctor Frankenstein and Herbert West could have performed their unspeakable experiments in very good company. It is a tragic, horrific, wonderful world long familiar to us from the writings of Verne, Burroughs, and Lovecraft.

And, indeed, Alex often draws direct inspiration from early weird fiction and its recurring theme of science pitted against the unknown, exploration against ignorance. "Many of my back-stories involve men and women who have turned away from superstition in the hope of finding solace in reason," he says. "My greatest passion is the unknown—ideas and things we wish to understand, but cannot."

It is the attempt to understand the ineffable that forms the core of Alex's art. It asks not only what *if*, but also what *is*—not always a comfortable question. Yet comfortable or not, somewhere deep in our twisted little hearts, don't we hope that all those wonderful worlds we have always dreamt of are really out there, just waiting to be discovered? Wouldn't we secretly all love to go there, even for a moment, no matter how frightening?

It's possible. It's not far at all. Alex has already packed you a case. ❧

A limited-edition pressing of *Many Dead Things: The Specimens of Lord Merrylin*, a photographic history of Alex CF's work, is available now on his Web site, with a wider printing to follow. Visit **www.alexcf.com** to pre-order.

Interview | BY SIMON THALMANN

ZOMBIES WITH BLASTERS?

*In a galaxy far, far away,
no one can hear you scream …*

I T'S BEEN AN especially good October for horror novelist Joe Schreiber, who released two new novels on the 13th: an original haunted-house tale, *No Doors, No Windows,* and the first all-out horror novel set in the *Star Wars* universe, *Death Troopers.* The latter has generated huge buzz, and the book's promoters have pulled out all the stops, giving it its own Web site, a tie-in "quest series" to the popular online game *Star Wars Galaxies* (marking the first time the game has introduced content inspired by a current novel), and an official StarWars.com "Zombie Week" featuring undead-themed *Star Wars* art. We caught up with Schreiber, 40, by phone to discuss *Death Troopers,* which follows the plight of the survivors on the *Purge,* an Imperial prison barge that breaks down in a distant, uninhabited part of space and comes across a seemingly abandoned Star Destroyer.

How does one transition from writing straight horror novels to writing a *Star Wars* horror novel? Like a lot of people my age, I grew up watching the original three movies, and I loved them, and I still love them. My editor at Del Rey and Ballantine was also involved in the *Star Wars* expanded universe books that they do, and there'd been a conversation with the office about how cool it would be to do a *Star Wars* horror novel, and they asked me if I would be interested in it, and I jumped at the chance … I definitely went about it with the idea of writing a book that you wouldn't necessarily have to be a huge fan of *Star Wars* to enjoy. I mean, you could read it as sort of a standalone horror or suspense novel; that was sort of my approach when I tackled it.

How was the writing process different using a preexisting world? It was ironically liberating, actually. They had an idea of when they wanted the book set, but other than that I really had pretty much free reign to do what I wanted to do . . . within the Lucas universe. It made it a lot of fun to do.

***Death Troopers* is set just before *A New Hope*. How does the book fit into that continuity? Are there Easter eggs?** There are definitely some familiar elements for people who love those first three movies. And it's a great sort of chronological sweet spot to have this occur . . . It's like the last great wild moment before all these iconic characters came together in that first *Star Wars* movie, so there's definitely stuff there you'll recognize.

You've said before that you thought the zombie genre, like the vampire genre, was being overdone. One of the cool things about the zombie genre, I think, is that you can do a lot with it. I mean, obviously zombie [stories] run the gamut, from *28 Days Later* to George Romero's movies, to all kinds of different. Basically any time you've got a group of people isolated against a larger marauding force, it sort of seems to fall within that bigger umbrella of the zombie novel. I don't want to give too much away for those who haven't read the book yet, but in the sense that you've got this apparently abandoned vessel with things living in it that present a great danger to the people who are there, it definitely fits within that bigger template of what we think of as a zombie book. I was careful to never use the phrase 'zombie' when I was writing. I feel like if you can pull away from that a little bit it actually makes it a little bit cooler.

It's interesting in that, watching the early movies especially, the Stormtroopers kind of have a zombie-like quality already; you don't really see their humanity. Does this book make room for troopers to be more human? I love that idea, and I never really thought of that consciously, but you're totally right. I mean, as a

CAROLE NELSON DOUGLAS

VAMPIRE SUNRISE

DELILAH STREET: PARANORMAL INVESTIGATOR

"Wonderfully written . . . A unique take on the paranormal." —*New York Times* bestselling author Kelley Armstrong

Werewolf mobsters & vampires run Vegas

• •

. . . but that's yesterday's news for Delilah Street, paranormal investigator. What's truly fearsome is her bloody discovery of an undead evil rooted in ancient Egypt. Now, with her lover Ric fighting for life after a grim battle, the chips are down.

"Douglas has populated her Post-Millenium Las Vegas with the most outrageous and outlandish cast of supporting characters this side of *The Wizard of Oz*.... The rich details and inventive mysteries . . . completely submerge you in the story." —SCIFIGUY

JUNO

POCKET BOOKS
A Division of Simon & Schuster
A CBS COMPANY

kid especially you see Stormtroopers operate in silence and they're kind of identical. They totally seem like zombies. But at the same time . . . in a lot of ways they're just infantryman. They sign up to serve the Empire; they're guys who put on armor and then at the end of the day take it off, so . . . you get to enjoy both the freaky anonymity of the Strormtrooper helmet but also the personalities of the guys who had to put the armor on and fight for the cause.

The *Star Wars* universe is incredibly popular. Did you feel pressure to make sure you got the minutiae right or you'd be jumped on by rabid fans? Yeah, definitely. Not in a negative sense, but very much in the sense that I'm dealing with something that's been pretty clearly diagrammed forward and backward, both by Lucasfilm and by the people who enjoy their work. So when I first said I would take the job, these big boxes of reference materials started showing up on my doorstep from Lucasfilm. I literally had a two-foot stack of reference guides next to my desk that I constantly was going through to make sure that I was not only getting the details right, but really sort of using it to its fullest potential as far as what's out there, because so much has been done . . . You try to stay away from some of what's on the bulletin boards, because online when the deal was first announced, for as many people as were excited about it there were some people who were just like, "This is just gonna suck! This is the worst idea ever!" I told my editor about that and he was like, "Yeah, you really just should stay away from that stuff."

Your novel *No Doors, No Windows* came out the same day as *Death Troopers*. Are you any more excited about one versus the other? It's a funny thing, because you just wear different hats. I mean, *No Doors, No Windows* took me several years to get to where it got published. Between edits and rewrites, that book's been sort of in the pipeline since about 2005—whereas the *Star Wars* thing, once I got the go-ahead for it, I had a couple of months to put it together. So one is definitely a more intense process of *work on it with no other distractions,* and the other is sort of like a kid that I've watched grow up. So you're like the parent who says, 'Oh, I love them both in different ways,' but that's basically true. I don't

necessarily feel more strongly about one than the other but I definitely feel differently as far as the process that spawned them.

Given that you worked on *No Doors, No Windows* so much longer, do you worry that the *Star Wars* book will overshadow it will all its publicity? You try to be realistic about it. I mean, honestly, my publisher has a lot more at stake with the *Star Wars* book, and I recognized that going in. They love both books, and my publicist wants to make sure both books get attention, but the reality is you're dealing with an audience of lots and lots of fans with the one—and with the other you're dealing with an audience that hopefully will enjoy it. It's coming out the same day, and when I tour, both of the books will be out there, and I hope people will pick the other up—you know, just because they're interested in *Star Wars*, and also the hope is that there

RECENT WEIRDNESS

TEMPEST RISING by Nicole Peeler (Hachette, $7.99) It's not every day you find out you're only half human— but that's the wake-up call Jane True gets one watery, winter night. Jane's discovery of her supernatural selkie heritage (one of urban fantasy's rarer myths!) opens the door to a seductive new world full of powerful vampires, healing dogs, and a dangerously tempting genie's lamp.

WORMWOOD, NEVADA by David Oppegaard (St. Martin's Press, $24.99) Nothing disrupts the bumbling sanctity of earthly existence like a visitor from space. In Oppegaard's latest, the invader in question is a meteorite that sets off a chain reaction of apocalyptic paranoia among Wormwood's doomsday prophets, alien cultists, meth dealers, and the poor couple at the heart of it all.

MADNESS OF FLOWERS by Jay Lake (Night Shade Books, $14.95) Battles may be fought and won, but greed and corruption will endure. Lake (who'll return to *WT* in the next issue!) approaches this fatalistic outlook with aplomb, filling *Madness* with adventure, political intrigue, and outlandish characters, including a godlike dwarf, a beautiful tomb raider, and a living dead man.

will be some horror fans who may try a *Star Wars* novel who might not have normally picked it up.

Is *No Doors, No Windows* a departure from your previous horror novels in any way? It's a bit of a departure in that my earlier two horror novels, *Chasing the Dead* and *Eat the Dark*, were definitely these full-throttle, right out of the gate, very streamlined horror novels. The idea was to strap you to a rocket in Chapter One and you'd look up at three in the morning and realize you just finished the whole book. And *No Doors, No Windows* was an attempt to try something maybe a little bit more ambitious, a haunted-house novel with more of a slow burn so that when the real horror of what's going on finally kicks in, you've created this atmosphere of dread that envelopes the reader.

Will you be reading from both on your current book tour? That's a really good question. I'm not sure. I guess it depends how many people show up wearing Stormtrooper helmets versus black shirts with skulls on them. I may have to make that decision when I get there. There's a few points of mutual cross-reference between the two books, so maybe I can find something . . . There's a scene in *No Doors, No Windows* where one of the guys is sitting at the bar and looks up and the bartender is reading this *Star Wars* book with a severed Stormtrooper's head on it, and he's like, "When did this whole world become about death?"

You have another *Star Wars* novel due out next year, as well as one based on the TV show *Super-natural*. Meanwhile, you moonlight working the midnight shift as an MRI tech near your home. Any plans to quit the "day" job and focus solely on writing? That's the question of the century. I talk to other people who've done stuff like that, who've worked their jobs and then tried to go to just writing, and at this point the best I could probably hope for is to cut the hours back at some point. Between the health insurance my job gives me and the financial security, at this point it probably would be more stressful to try to go full time writing. But I haven't taken my eye off that, obviously. That's sort of the Grail . . . you gotta dream big. ☺

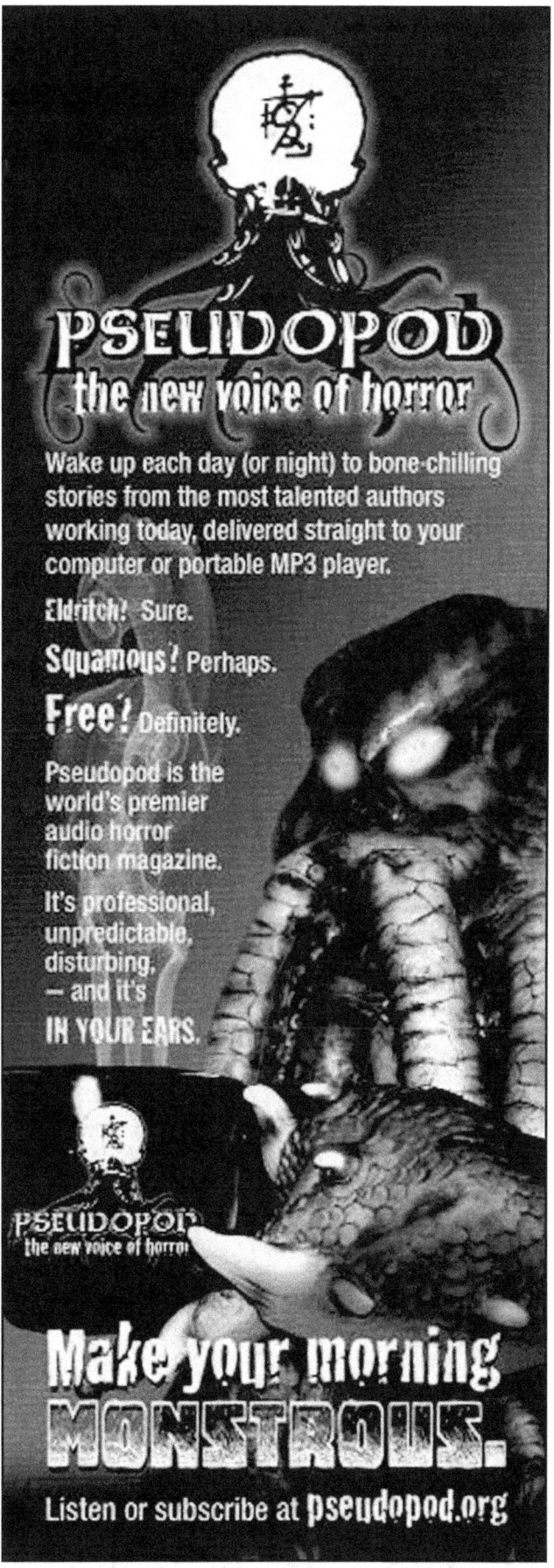

PSEUDOPOD
the new voice of horror

Wake up each day (or night) to bone-chilling stories from the most talented authors working today, delivered straight to your computer or portable MP3 player.

Eldritch? Sure.

Squamous? Perhaps.

Free? Definitely.

Pseudopod is the world's premier audio horror fiction magazine.

It's professional, unpredictable, disturbing, — and it's

IN YOUR EARS.

PSEUDOPOD
the new voice of horror

Make your morning MONSTROUS.

Listen or subscribe at pseudopod.org

GROWING UP POE

Edgar Allan Poe would be celebrating his 200th birthday this year. He cast an epic shadow across American fiction; he inspired every last horror writer who came after him; and his fans founded this very 'zine. WEIRD TALES wondered if Poe still has the same impact today—so we asked a bevy of dark fantasists how much the Grandpa of the Gothic loomed in their tender years. The answer: a whole freakin' lot.

ILLUSTRATION BY ALEX ECKMAN-LAWN

LEAKY GRAVES

BY RAMSEY SHEHADEH

I'M STANDING ON a small stage in a big classroom in Bethesda, Maryland. I'm 17. A sparse crowd of teenagers, sprawled on folding chairs, are staring up at me with expressions that range from desperate boredom to mild, grudging shock.

I'm screaming at them.

Specifically, I'm screaming this:

"O God! what COULD I do? I foamed—I raved—I swore! I swung the chair upon which I had been sitting, and grated it upon the boards, but the noise arose over all and continually increased. It grew louder—louder—louder! And still the men chatted pleasantly, and smiled. Was it possible they heard not? Almighty God!—no, no?"

Which is to say, I'm giving a dramatic reading of *The Tell-Tale Heart*. The beating of the old man's heart, buried with the rest of him beneath the floorboards, has finally pushed his murderer over the edge, and he will soon tell the police what he's done. The performance calls for some mad eye-rolling, a little rending of clothes, loads of unhinged raving, and the occasional vigorous spate of lectern-pounding.

"They heard!" I wail. "They suspected!—they KNEW!—they were making a mockery of my horror!"

Portions of my little audience are certainly making a mockery of something, but it isn't my horror. The unfortunate girl sitting in the front row, well within spittle range of my acting spasms, has her head in her hand, and is trembling slightly with something that is not, I assure myself, laughter.

This is speech class, and we've been asked to give a reading from our favorite stories. I didn't have to think too hard about what I wanted to do. Back then, Poe was my man. I had a giant omnibus edition of his

"The Tell-Tale Heart" calls for some mad eye-rolling, a little rending of clothes, and loads of unhinged raving.

collected work at home, and spent a really unhealthy amount of time poring over its myriad unpleasantnesses. The poems I mostly left alone, because poetry was for girls, but the stories were a revelation: a cramped suffocating claustrophobic revelation, yes, but nevertheless an endlessly fascinating window into the troubling depths of the human mind.

I didn't give it much thought, then, but it seems in retrospect like an odd thing for a youngish person to be obsessed with. The trajectory of early life is defiantly *outwards*, a symbolic extension of that first escape from the womb. We spend a lot of time trying to get away from the inside of our own heads. But Poe's fiction represents the exact opposite of this impulse. It's relentlessly, pathologically, *inward*, peopled with characters who are forever burying each other in dark, improvised graves.

Graves that are, all too often, insufficient to the task. Whether it's a stubbornly beating heart or a bricked-up cat or the dank subterranean pricklings of conscience, Poe's internments always seem to be springing inconvenient leaks. It doesn't matter if you take these stories at face value, or see in them the dark atrocities of a mind at war with itself: the inescapable message here is that we can't rid ourselves of the worst aspects of our nature. Because those things aren't just a part of us—they *are* us. Even if we succeed in hiding them from the world, we can't hide them from ourselves.

"But anything was better than this agony!" I scream—feeling, now, that I'm speaking for the whole class, whose amusement has lapsed back into sardonic ennui. My

strategy of substituting volume for insight seems to be failing, at least partly because this material really isn't suited to bellowing— its claustrophobic brand of sensationalism is an interior thing, a crawling-into-your-own-head thing. It's a dark funhouse mirror, reflecting the worst parts of all who read it.

So why on earth *does* anyone read it? Our culture's preference for escapist fiction is pretty well-documented (in box office returns, if nothing else) and much of Poe's stuff is anything but escapism. So what's going on?

My guess is that we actually *want* to look in that mirror, if only to make sure that we don't recognize too much of ourselves in it. There's a definite there-but-for-the-grace-of-sanity dimension to the thrill you get from reading these stories. Which is, I think, the hallmark of all good horror. I'm as much a fan of Cthulhu-esque pandimensional abomination fiction as they next guy, but for *real* scares there's nothing like the specter of the mind betraying itself. Because the worst demons—maybe the *only* demons—are the ones that live inside our skin.

"Villains!" I shriek, "dissemble no more! I admit the deed!—tear up the planks!—here, here!—it is the beating of his hideous heart!"

Thus ends my dramatic reading.

There's a brief silence, followed by perfunctory applause, all limned in a giant nimbus of desperate relief. I step off the stage, and go back to my seat. I chewed up about all the available scenery, which is a kind of accomplishment, I suppose—but otherwise the whole thing was a pretty mortifying failure. No acting career was launched that day.

Which I'm okay with, in retrospect. You don't want to get too close to Poe. I'm quite content to stand back and admire his dark genius from afar. It's a nice place to visit, as they say. But I wouldn't want to be buried there.

Ramsey Shehadeh splits his time between writing stories and writing software. He blogs at doodleplex.com.

PHOTO BY CTACIK

GROWING UP POE

TEEN ANGEL, DARK

BY ALETHEA KONTIS

FOURTEEN: THE AGE of nihilistic fervor. The pinnacle of those egocentric, life-altering years where no one suffered as much as me. In a million years no one could possibly have understood the ineffable quagmire of emotions in which I flailed, a lone gull crying out over the empty seas of my tears. To make matters worse (because matters could always be worse, and usually were), the innocence of youth had left me with the tiniest flicker of hope, and a dream that the brooding prince of a tiny, heretofore-unknown kingdom (who, coincidentally, happened to be my One True Love) would come galloping by on his horse at any moment to save me from the hell that was my life. He would see through the physical mess I had become and know the Real Me, the beautiful, shining beacon of soul held hostage by my own darkness. But alas! the newly-forged, freshly-jaded adult side of my Mini-Wheat knew that there was no such prince. No one was coming for me. Hope was futile. I was doomed to be left behind by the world, forever alone, a small, forgotten puddle of disappointment, darkness, and despair.

Enter Poe. And The Cure.

Life had a soundtrack in those days. The radio played songs chock-full of hidden messages, battered symphonies of secrets whispered only for my tortured ears. Volumes could be read into mixtapes that were as personal as journal entries, telling the story

of my duality, my constant struggle between darkness and light. I wore my heart on my sleeve, freely dripping blood down hallways and hoping someone would notice. (That brooding prince, maybe.) I had been writing poetry since I was ten—almost a third of my life. I was in love with the power of words, the ability to say so much with so little. It was a gift—I had a gift—and I would not squander it.

Music was the logical next step in poetry's evolution, but I was not a lyricist. Sure, I had walked around the house singing nonsense tunes as a child, but I lacked the genius code in my DNA attributed to such luminaries as Rodgers & Hammerstein, Gilbert & Sullivan, and the virtuoso that was Cole Porter. I would never be a songwriter. That didn't mean, however, that I couldn't lie corpse-like on my bed in a room soaked in dusk (and wallpapered in movie posters) and appreciate the talents of Robert Smith or Peter Cetera or Bryan Adams. I was that small-town girl in her lonely world, bags packed for that midnight train to anywhere (preferably an equally small, heretofore-unknown kingdom). My hurt didn't show, but the pain still grew. Me & Charles Manson liked the same ice cream. I was a strange angel, an angel of music, and the Phantom of the Opera was there, inside my mind.

Any member of the Spring Valley Players worth his or her salt knew all the words to Andrew Lloyd Weber's production of *Phantom* (though I was the only one who could sing Christine's part). Memorization is what we did in those days. After all, if I was going to be Lights Mistress, I had to know every line of *See How They Run* in order to hit all my cues. Every line . . . including the first verse of "If," by Rudyard Kipling. And when I found the rest of the poem in a set of Kipling's works at my grandmother's house that summer, I soaked it up. I was a sponge that could not be saturated. It was the beginning of the end.

I started memorizing all sorts of poetry after that, starting with the poems that had any excuse to be in one of our plays ("The Jabberwocky"). I memorized fun stuff with my little sister as a game—Shel Silverstein, of course, and the often-quoted-but-rarely-attributed Ogden Nash, of whom we were both great fans at a very young age (we liked mustard, even on custard). But the best part about memorizing poetry was when I got to play the role of the overachieving student. (There's nothing like having fun and getting extra credit for it!) Shakespeare? No problem. Sonnets, Friends, Romans, Countrymen, and star-

SIX WAKING NIGHTMARES POE GAVE ME IN THIRD GRADE

BY MIKE ALLEN

1 At night, the light fixture above my bed stretched into a pale blue vulture eye, and the emaciated ghost of the man it belonged to swirled out, craggy face contorted in silent accusation as he reached for me, but—

2 I didn't dare turn my head, for fear of the man with the toothsome smile who would emerge from my closet and disassemble himself like a thing made of paper tabs and glue, and what he would look like as he kept crawling towards me. Yet—

3 If I shut my eyes, the old man would never leave me alone, the pounding I heard not the pulse of blood in my ears but the beat of his heart, thumping, thumping, thumping, as he lay dismembered beneath my bed, and—

crossed lovers separated by only a balcony. Byron, anyone? Oh, the sappier the better.

Unfortunately, two of my favorite poems—"The Highwayman" and "The Raven"—were both far too long, and I would not be a complete person (as complete as I could be, imperfect soul though I was) without some Poe in my repertoire. There must be *something* else in my literature book. And there, buried deep in the back, I met Annabel Lee.

Known as Poe's Last Poem, "Annabel Lee" was beautiful and sad, true and tragic. It spoke to me, telling me a tale of a love

that was more (more!) than love, a love that made even heaven jealous, the one love that lasts a lifetime . . . albeit a very, very short lifetime. Obviously, the only kind of love I could possibly be destined to have, and currently, um, *did not.* I was covetous alongside those angels, craving such pure, rare, unprecedented, unadulterated feeling and dying a little inside their immortal souls to know they could not let it exist on the mortal plane. I read the first line out loud to myself, "It was many and many a year ago," Poe's Once Upon a Time. And suddenly the strangest thing happened: the poem began singing itself to me in my head.

I had never before composed a song (and likely never will again), but the words of that ballad of true love, tempests, and tragedy had an unmistakable melody that I remember to this day. It was as if Poe Himself sat at the foot of his bride's tomb and sang to me a song only I could hear, a tune that traveled beyond time. It was sad, that song; I belted it out full voice in empty rooms, a nightingale calling in the nighttide. Perhaps many and many a year ago I had been Annabel Lee, the maiden from a tiny, heretofore-unknown kingdom by the sea, and Poe was my brooding prince. Because of the intensity of our love we could never again cohabit the mortal plane (as all men know). But he could send me the tale of our love through the bond that would always remain between our souls, and I would always carry in my heart this song we made together.

Or not.

Now that I'm grown, I chalk all that up to the silliness of youth, the alien angst we all go through. But I'd be lying if I said that part of me—a very, very small part—didn't still pine a bit for the Poe I never knew. But I still have our song.

4 If I kept my eyes shut, I would feel the deadly rush of air as that long curved blade swung from above, swept lower and lower as I lay wrapped and trapped in my blankets. I could never, ever sleep, and—

5 If I did, I would wake up buried, faceless men dumping dirt on me from above as I screamed in my coffin, smothered and alone with the gold bugs that bit and the deathwatch beetles and hideous throngs of conqueror worms. But—

6 None of it mattered, no matter how many nights I stayed awake and afraid, because soon the great raven that hid in every shadow would pluck out my pale and fluttering soul, and I knew then I would nevermore see happiness or Heaven.

Nebula Award-nominated writer **Mike Allen** edits the *Clockwork Phoenix* anthology series.

Alethea Kontis is a *New York Times* bestselling author, editor, essayist, interviewer, fairy princess, and geek.

GROWING UP POE

THE VIRTUES OF THE DEAD

BY CHERIE PRIEST

MY FATHER SAYS that my mother wasn't always the Evangelical weirdo I grew up with, but I don't have any proof to the contrary so it's difficult for me to imagine. All I know for certain is that by the time I was old enough to read, fiction was a dangerous gamble—because Mom's guidelines for acceptable reading were fluid, odd, and sometimes arbitrary.

For example, during the 1980s there was a trend in Christian fiction toward stories of white pioneer women getting raped and creatively mutilated by filthy godless Indians on the prairie. As far as my mother was concerned, those stories were just dandy. She owned scores of them. And since, in the end, Jesus always triumphed so the good guys went to heaven, these books fell into the category of Perfectly Wholesome Reading Material for Third-Graders.

But the Nancy Drew stories I brought home from the library were thrown in the trash, to be paid for out of my own meager allowance. Apparently I should have known better than to invite the presence of Satan into our home. I'd like to pretend I'm kid-

ding, and that she didn't say this out loud in front of God, the librarians, and everybody, but alas. I'm not, and she *did*.

As I grew older and better able to hide books, my leisure reading became a battleground where my by-then-divorced parents could fight without bloodshed. Dad figured out that I was a big fan of mysteries, ghosts, and monsters; Mom figured it out too, and she subsequently became hyper-vigilant of my bookbag, lest I introduce any of this heathen nonsense into her austere Protestant temple.

But there was an escape clause: Dead authors were okay.

(Does this make any sense? No, no it does not. But my mother also believed that men who could do splits were likely in league with the devil, and that doesn't make any sense either. Many things in my childhood can therefore be taken with a grain of salt.)

My dad got crafty, and one Christmas I received a *Complete Tales and Works of Edgar Allan Poe*. I was ten years old, and it was the single largest book I, personally, had ever owned. It could've sunk a canoe. I could barely lift it, so I mostly read it lying down—on my bed, chin in hands and feet flapping happily while I pored through some of the coolest, bleakest, darkest, most engaging stories I'd ever encountered.

Oh, I still loved Nancy Drew—and I still snuck the small yellow hardbacks home from the library, sometimes down my pants, if necessary; but I had a new Most Important Writer in my life. He was a sad-eyed man wearing old clothes and a sour mustache, and he wrote about beautiful women with supernatural wasting diseases, and talking birds who foretold doom. He told stories about peril and tragedy, and addiction and loss. He wrote elaborately and thickly, and passionately and profoundly, and I adored him from the bottom of my black little heart.

Poe was my first introduction to truly strange secular literature.

He was the first author who ever told me that it was okay to tell dark, sad little stories and take them seriously—and that

ILLUSTRATION BY MOLLY CRABAPPLE

furthermore, that this was the only way to write them. I took heart from his insistence all through high school, when I doodled scary tales in notebooks that nobody saw; I leaned on it at the private Christian college I attended, where horror and fantasy were not so much encouraged; and I clung to it in graduate school, where I was told that genre fiction of all kinds was trash, and no one should ever bother with it, least of all me and certainly not in a respectable workshop filled with upstanding students who damn well knew better than to write such drivel.

So thank you, Edgar.

Thank you for refusing to apologize, and for the pride you took in your work—critics be damned. You set a great example for me, and you'll always have a soft spot in my heart, and on my bookshelf.

Cherie Priest's latest novel is *Boneshaker*.

HOW COME I WRITE HORROR

BY ALEXANDRA ELIZABETH HONIGSBERG

THE SNOW FELL heavily, so that even the tank-like red '57 Chevy had a rough time pushing on through to Brooklyn Hospital. But finally it got there and fulfilled its mission, welcoming the firstborn of a Sicilian-Italian immigrant clan's second generation. She was born to scared twentysomething parents from Gravesend, and she was born among strangers, in white-'n-chrome antiseptic assembly-line fashion, covered in fine dark fur like some baby beast and beset by purple boils. The fur fell off after a few days. The boils were treated with purple antiseptic paint, gentia violet, and prayers to St. Christopher and the Virgin Mary, and some of the marks have lasted a lifetime.

The world she was born into was part space age, part Middle Ages. Sputnik and spores. Atomic Armageddon. Duck and cover. Vaccines were mostly nonexistent, and thus she got nearly every plague a child could suffer, yet somehow survived. Medicine was still rather primitive— tonsils were ripped out of children's throats with hooks while they were strapped into black doctor's-office chairs, chlorophormed, told to shut up; teeth torn out of young mouths with pliers by guys with big hairy hands and little or no anesthesia. Benjamin Spock hadn't yet written his groundbreaking childcare book, so corporal punishment was considered a God-driven necessity, lest kids grow up to be hoodlums, go to jail, and die. And Planned Parenthood was still a new, godless wonder, so, a mere 20 months after a firstborn girl, it was not unusual for the next child to arrive, a successful try for a son to carry on the dad's name—a sickly little boy, and thus the girl then gets thrown out of her crib to a big-girl's bed with unpadded brass railings, and is set in the role of caretaker big sister and surrogate mom that would define her for the rest of her days, if she didn't escape in time. Sicilians were called niggers by other Italians; those boogeymen, the Mafia, ruled large swaths of New York City's grassroots industries; and the majority of good-guy Italians just tried to work, feed their families, and make their mamas proud—but hey, don't do *too* much better than your fathers did, lest you emasculate them. Mothers with mental health issues were given shock treatments and committed to places worthy of Boris Karloff, left slack-jawed and raccoon-eyed in the name of healing, finally to come home eerily sweet—but prone to turning horrifically violent in an instant, their triggers unknown. Poe would've been proud. In such a milieu, one could easily be buried alive, behind cultural and institutional brick walls. *For the love of God, Montresor!*

This was me. This was my family. This was what I, a future horror writer, was born into. And things only got stranger as I got older. The Middle Ages persisted even as the Age of Aquarius dawned, and these two spheres, the darkness and the light, warred throughout my life—sometimes comically, sometimes tragically. It's always made for good story, with the names changed to protect the innocent, the guilty, the human.

My late Mom—in fact, all my relatives—always asked me, "How come you write horror?" They shouldn't have needed to ask. It was Grandma herself who named me *strega*—witch!—because I'd been caught meditating on roses in her garden at the age of four and, just two years later, dared to question the patriarchal nature of the priesthood 'cause, after all, "Mary was a girl."

I have a vivid imagination. This is its own reward, its own blessing. Still, horror always accompanies it.

THE IMAGERY CAME early and often, unbidden, real and surreal. There are memories that I'm not supposed to be able to recall, from when I was younger than two, and yet I do recall them in all their visceral details—like the tonsillectomy, with its abduction and Big Nurse's threats and my kicking and screaming to not go gentle into what I'd feared would be that good night, "God will punish you!" But there are better memories, too. I was seven, amidst rows of paired-off little girls and boys dressed in white, as if for a wedding, prayerbooks and rosary beads in hand; the girls veiled, Brides of Christ. There was all the pomp and circumstance that an Italian Roman Catholic parish in Queens could muster: shiny vestments, fragrant incense, organ blaring, and all of us chanting in Latin. I knew what it meant. All of it. It was *magic*. It tied together times and places that were near and far, alien and yet intimately familiar. This is how it'd been for nearly a millennium. This is how I'd hoped it would always be—but Vatican II took away some of the mystery the very next year, and I felt the loss. My faith was deep and simple: God is good, Satan is bad, saints are extraordinary people, prayer works, miracles happen. What more did I need to know?

By Grandma's house where Dad had grown up on the unfashionable side of Park Slope, near the trainyard, there stands historic Green-Wood Cemetery—full of people picnicking, musicians playing, ponds with

ILLUSTRATION BY LORELYN MEDINA

swans my family has fed for five generations, mausoleums fit to be aristocratic homes, and a gorgeous Tiffany-glassed chapel. Though it is associated with death, it is a place of life, and the two co-existed between the fountains and angel statues, a dance of the arts never ending in this kingdom by the sea. Today, my beloved husband is buried there, near Leonard Bernstein and Charles Ebbets, and I will join him, someday, I know not when. The hills overlook the harbour, and I know full well how the frosty winds can come out of a cloud by night, chilling and killing the beautiful Annabel Lee, as Mom had read me Poe's poems and stories at bedtime since I was very young. I often wonder if Mom, through the intermittent fogs of her illness, was unconsciously trying to tell me something through those wintry tales. But I don't mind the grey, between the candle and the darkness, though I also love the riot of colour that is that memorial park in full bloom. It is soothing, soft, safe, peaceful, old.

Safety is an illusion, maybe even a delusion, fleeting and perhaps nonexistent. But I search for it like the Holy Grail nonetheless. Often I search for it in people, trusting soul that I can be. You'd think you'd be safe with your elders. They could be the most unsafe creatures in the universe, full of their own monsters, whether by mental illness or just terminal cluelessness. A tree-lined playground becomes a battlefield when you're surrounded by hostile gangs of grade-school kids. Then you swing your lunchbox to keep them away and the metal edge cuts one of them, unintentionally, and an elder comes to stop things, and you think you're saved. But suddenly you're on trial as a demon-child for violent behaviour, and scores of witnesses perjure themselves, and no one else is held accountable and no one believes you and you're sure they're going to press you to death under stones for your transgressions. For being different. *She's precocious! She writes stories! She questions her elders! She makes things up!* That's what they say. But you're innocent! Well, you are a witch, and it is time for your trial.

Or you have your first teenaged boyfriend over to a home Halloween party with all your friends and sibs—your parents just upstairs—and he presses you for sex, and you say no, and he won't walk away, and it takes three other guys to pull him off of you as he has you trapped in your own laundry room in your own basement, pressed against the washing machine, cold and hard and cruel. They throw him out, and he curses you. Something in you shrinks away from those words, those eyes, but you eventually forget about it—till there's this demon that shows up after midnight at Girl Scout camp in the mountains, middle of nowhere, beautiful, dark, chthonic . . . no, it's not a bear . . . other campers and counselors saw it, too, but the grownups hush it up, saying the girl telling

the story is a "troublemaker" and "too emotional." No one believes you in public, but late at night, in private, you hear the whispers: what they heard and saw, the burnt footprints on the trail, the destroyed God's Eyes and crosses all over the campsite, the rancid stream that'd never had a problem before the sightings. And you read a *Newsday* article that says your crazy ex-boyfriend is studying with Long Island's most notorious self-proclaimed black warlock, and you remember the curse and put the pieces together and shudder every night for years. But time softens the fear and you go to college, fulfill your dreams, leave the madness and evil of banal suburban Long Island for a new life of your own making and choosing—until the ghost hunters come to town, and you go to the program because you think it's going to be interesting. Later, you look at their book and drop it to the floor with a gasp when there on the page before you stares the demon you saw at camp five years earlier. They believe you, the ghost hunters do, but they want to use you as bait to call the horror back. You run.

I didn't know if they could do what they said they could do, but I didn't want to find out, and I still don't. I hid in the arms of my new beloved and the riot of fall colours and my music and, eventually, images of the bad boy and the demon went away.

LIFE WENT ON, and the beloved and I made our fairy tales come true in many ways—a spring garden wedding in full Renaissance and *Gone With the Wind* garb included. Once again I was read to at night: not Poe this time, but funny stories, fantastical stories, mystical poetry. And I read on my own, too. We had very little, we twentysomething artsy romantics, but we had everything. Books were our constant companions, our sense of wonder, and we studied and studied, going back to our faiths, Hebrew and Latin and Greek and all the ancient sacred languages, all the people's stories, full of magic and miracles, mortals and myths. And the mystical was our home: real Kabbalah, alchemy, the

Western esoteric tradition, Arthuriana.

We moved just down the street from the Cloisters and that became Home, complete with Mother Cabrini's dead body in the crystal altar in her shrine just across the street. We joined with like-minded people and studied and debated, back to the Middle Ages in a good way, like the ancient universities. We stood circles together, drew down the moon, comforted the bereaved, healed the sick, did pathworkings, and walked the Labyrinth to know God and know ourselves.

And we dared to ask for the truth.

In one prayer circle during the first Gulf War of '91, we asked for wisdom and protection for all those involved on both sides, and we mentally strove to project that love and strength to our human brothers and sisters in Iraq. On the far perimeter of our senses during the group meditation, two of us spontaneously rushed ahead in visualization to meet our faraway brethren—and next we knew, we were jerked back to the here and now as our bodies were literally *knocked on our asses.* No one knew what'd just happened; we were okay, but we could've been harmed and we knew it. Later that weekend we read in a *Times* article that Saddam Hussein claimed to be employing black magicians to guard the perimeter of his palace. Connect the dots. I'd already seen stranger.

Foolish child that I was, even in my thirties, I dared to do that again in the Labyrinth, and so a vision was revealed to me of the biblical Jacob's Ladder and my infinitesimal tininess in Infinity. My fellow pilgrims said that I was lost in the center for an hour; they didn't see me and I certainly wasn't seeing them, though it had seemed but a moment. And then I was back, just like that. Who knows what happened and how? But it's an image, a memory I hold, along with my simple faith that is more complex than I can comprehend. After a lifetime of having dreams that would come true, of not needing Caller ID to know who

was on the phone before they said hello, and of sensing when someone had died, I learned to accept the things I cannot understand—to learn and keep seeking, even when it scared me and left me breathless.

I'd learned that from the horror movies I'd watched with Dad all through my childhood, too. Accept and plan accordingly. Understanding may come later. Or it may not.

THE STORMS I'D been born into continued, but in the midst of them I now heard the small, still voice of my simple faith: "Be a priest." After much doubt, denying the call three times in biblical fashion, having myself tested for psychoses and, to my relief, being told that I had not inherited that family legacy, I accepted it. I would bring magic to people. Good magic.

I went to seminary in New York and lectured at Christ Church at Oxford—yes, Hogwarts, literally and figuratively! I searched for my Philosopher's Stone and faced the Chambre of Secrets, the Goblet of Fire, and the Deathly Hallows. And finally, when I was ready, I escaped Azkaban and the Dementers and Death-Eaters, joined the Order of the Phoenix, and worked with Dumbledore to save the world, taking summers off with my equivalent of the Dursleys and spending Christmas and Chanukah with my dear Cuban Weasleys.

And then, in undue time, we lost our crew's Dumbledore, our Gandalf, my beloved, to some freak biological glitch, the horror of the moment still fresh in my mind, trying to save him and failing and watching his spirit disappear from his eyes, on a perfectly ordinary spring morning, set to do ordinary things, blue sky, safe at home with the cat.

Every horror story has at least one major character casualty and one who's left to carry on. Every romance. This is mine, through laughter and tears, the totally mundane and the utterly unbelievable, in every season.

This is how come I write horror. ☺

Ambient Morgue Music

BY RICHARD HOWARD

ILLUSTRATION BY DAVID PROSSER

IN WHICH OUR

CORRESPONDENT

IN IRELAND

REPORTS A VERY

ODD DISCOVERY

THE BEST THING about being a reviewer is that you often receive music in the old fashioned way, via a CD through your letterbox. Anyone jaded with this century's downloading obsession and its associated esoterica of bit rates, compressions and conversions will no doubt be turning snot-coloured with envy at this point. [*Oh, the quaint and glamorous life you lead ... Ed.*] Yes, I actually receive music through the post with handwritten covers, illustrations, bribes, pleas, death threats ... and on top of that, the music is good.

Yes, it seems that only now in the 2030s is the true charact   e   r of this millennium's sound finally being heard. It's early days yet but, for my money, the best stuff is being made right here, in Dublin. I know that looking at most mags these days you wouldn't know it, but most of this music is being made far away from the hubris of the mainstream music business, by the disenfranchised, who can barely afford to eat, never mind pay a publicity agent. My favourite music of the last six months has, for the most part, arrived unexpectedly in my hallway like a burglar, a begging letter, a Halloween firework.

Ambient Morgue Music is one I look forward to in particular. There have been four volumes so far, arriving monthly, each accompanied with a black-and-white photograph of a corpse and a handful of soil. The track names, listed on the back, speak of bloody revolution, disease and, for reasons that will become clear later on, zoo animals. The music itself is an eerie type of lo-fi ambient; at times it's hard to make out the music from the microphone hiss, but I presume that that's part of the aesthetic, the sound of the room putting you right where they want you. It's beautifully hypnotic, filled with dread and, as I found out this week, truly revolutionary.

The only contact information provided is a mobile phone number and it changes with every dispatch. Since the first *Ambient Morgue*'s arrival I've been trying desperately to contact the artist or artists, but each time the phone has either been disconnected or I get the generic answering machine drone. Last week I finally made a connection.

"Hello." —A thick Dublin accent.

"Hello, you sent me some CDs. I really think they're great; would I be able to meet you and have a chat? I'd like to do a piece on them."

"Yeah de CD, ye like it yeah?"

"I think it's some of the best music being made at the moment."

"Okay, which one are you? Whereabouts are ye?"

"I'm living on North Circular Road."

"Ah sure, yer only five minutes up the road. Sure come up now if ye like. Ye know where the Phoenix is. Just gis a shout when yer at the monument."

My brain froze for a second. "Um… yeah, okay. I'll give you a ring when I get there."

Why had I never been to the Phoenix Park before? I've lived on North Circular Road for almost ten years, but I had never turned right upon leaving my house, always

left towards Phibsboro. Sometimes if I was walking into the city I'd cross the road and follow the picturesque houses of Oxmantown road, before turning left and strolling through Stoneybatter, towards the River Liffey. Why had I never chosen to take my walk in one of the largest city parks in the world? Come to think of it, why does nobody I know ever talk about it, let alone go there? My head swam with these, and many other questions, as I threw on my winter coat. Leaving the house I turned right, feeling slightly askew.

It was twilight as I made my way up the road. I looked around for something to keep me grounded in what I had come to believe was reality; I fixed on the trees, trying to ignore the colossal monument coming into view. Surely I'd have noticed something of that size at the end of the road I lived on.

I entered the park and followed the winding path to the monument. I took out my phone, but there was no need. He found me. An ordinary-looking young man, smartly dressed but slightly disheveled.

"Story bud?" The easy, familiar colloquialism took the edge off the uneasy, illusory feeling that had grown inside me since leaving my house.

"Hello, pleased to meet you." I offered my hand and we shook solidly.

He introduced himself as Dessy and then walked away, gesturing that I should follow him.

Reader, in my youth I enjoyed reading the fiction of the fantastical. Future dystopian nightmares, journeys to the stars and magickal conspiracies, I devoured them all. Bearing this in mind, I would have thought that what I'm about to explain would have been that much easier to comprehend. But, for all the reading in my youth of the classics of imaginative fiction, I was still left with nothing to compare with what unfolded over the next hour or so, beginning with the sight that startled me as we stood on top of that hill. On the area around the monument in the Phoenix Park I saw what I can only describe as a shantytown.

My stomach turned in giddy dread. I was so taken aback that Dessy had to let me stand for a while to take it in, my brain processing and reprocessing, programming and reprogramming. It was mind-blowing enough to be standing in a colossal green area in the middle of the city that had been completely erased from my consciousness like an early morning dream, but this threatened to smother my wits altogether. Rows and rows of dilapidated huts as far as I could see were broken here and there by mud tracks. Campfires burned. I could see people, too, going about their business as if following a daily routine. The atmosphere was one that my mind had never experienced, but that my body recalled, something primal and buried. How could this place, situated right in Dublin City, remain unremarked on by society?

I hadn't much time to entertain such a question, as Dessy beckoned me to follow him and we started down the hill towards the town. I trailed behind him, my head a swarm of ideas. As we got closer I realized that the scene I'd been viewing from the hill was less rustic than I'd first assumed. Everyone appeared reasonably well-groomed and fed; the men, women and children all wore modern clothing; and the children played with toys, handheld games and bikes that placed them firmly in the center of the twenty-first century. The huts themselves, on the other hand, were made from the kind of materials I would imagine have been employed for such purposes for over a hundred years: corrugated iron, tin, loose wood, plastic sheeting, cardboard and old furniture all converged to create the bric-a-brac village we stepped through. I saw a deer being roasted over an upturned shopping trolley and then remembered reading about the deer of Phoenix Park when I was young—a realization both nostalgic and grisly given the circumstances.

Seeing the flames licking around that beast's carcass served me well in one way, though, as I began to come to my senses

somewhat and my journalistic instincts began to kick in. How did these people get here? Why had nobody ever heard of them? Where was the music made? As we walked further these turned into questions about self-preservation. What did they intend to do with me? Was the music just a ruse to kidnap a member of the press?

We stopped at another campfire. Thankfully this one didn't contain any recently deceased wildlife, just a handful of men and women warming themselves against the intense cold. Dessy took me to the far side of the fire and introduced me to a man called Sean, who signaled for me to sit down on a cushion by the fire. Dessy disappeared.

"Now, what would you like to know?" said Sean, scratching his ample beard and staring right into my eyes.

"Um," I stuttered, taking a second to switch fully back into journalist mode, apparent cosmonaut that I'd become. "Well, how did you get here?"

The light from a fire has a way of changing one's appearance at every moment but, at a guess, I'd say Sean was in his mid-forties. I studied his jovial, friendly face as he mulled over the question.

"The government," he said finally.

"That's it? The government?"

"The Olympics," he said, and I fidgeted on my cushion, seriously considering walking away. He must have noticed the germ of my impatience, and he began shaking his head apologetically.

"I'm sorry,'" he said. "After all, we are the ones who have always known. You are the ones who have never known."

I settled back down as he continued.

"You do remember the Olympics, don't you?" He didn't wait for an answer. "Twenty years ago that bloody thing came to our city. Thousands of people forcibly removed from their homes to make way for the Olympic village, the new stadium, twelve-story car parks." He spat into the fire at the memory. "We were promised houses out in the suburbs—well, they call them suburbs—might

as well be outer space."

"So you sought refuge here?"

"Some of us sought refuge, others were chased here. We fought pitched battles with the police all the way up North Circular Road. Caused quite a stir at the time. At one point it looked like St. Peter's Church was going to go up in flames. Don't know how I would have explained that one to him at the Pearly Gates. Hopefully the pigs found a way to erase it from that document, too. Haha." His laugh turned into a cough and he spat again. The fire sizzled. "Of course some of us were already here, but the numbers were small so nobody really took any notice. Forced removal had been going on since the late nineteen hundreds and those that didn't want to go usually came here. That caused a bit of resentment at first, because since the newcomers, everybody's trapped here."

"Trapped?"

"Yes. From what we can gather, it's some kind of gravity field. If we try to leave it just propels us back. There are only three people in the whole camp that it doesn't affect. Dessy is one of them. The rest of us can't even pass the monument."

"But how?"

"It was the Olympic games. Every major technological country in the world had an interest in the games running smoothly. The amount of technology Ireland would have had at its disposal would have been unprecedented."

"But what about everyone else . . . outside . . ."

He just shrugged his shoulders and said, "But sure, isn't it the music you came here for? Come on."

We walked until the huts began to thin out, and I got a twitch of recall as in the distance I saw a naggingly familiar sign: DUBLIN ZOO.

"I haven't been here in . . ." I let the sentence trail off, giving in to what now appeared to be a full-scale hallucination. Deciding to jump onto surer ground, I began questioning him about the music as we pushed through the gates.

"So how did you make the music?"

"Gas."

I shook off his obvious flippancy and persisted with my questioning, "How do you record it?"

"My only inheritance was a suitcase full of microphones. My Dad used to record bands years and years ago. He was always buying microphones. He loved sound, god bless him and not much else . . . I just use them and an old computer . . ."

I had followed him into what used to be the reptile house.

"Don't worry," he said, switching on a light, "most of the animals are long dead. At the height of the battle we released a lot of them and charged the cops. The rhinos and hippos caused the most mayhem, not to mention the big cats. They were all gunned down in the end, of course. I feel terrible about that, but we made the choice. We did what we thought we had to do. Anyway, do you like it? My home studio."

I looked around the former reptile house with the same awe that visited me atop that hill. Memories started to awaken, doors unlocked in my brain that someone evidently wanted closed forever. At that point I remembered this place, reader, even if you do not. I remembered the crocodile, the iguana and the snakes but they were gone. Each case had been turned into a recording booth, with microphones hanging from the ceiling; the largest case contained a mixing desk and a computer. Even stranger, though, was when I came in for a closer look at the booths and saw the dead body lying on a slab in each one. Sean saw the look on my face and laughed a maniac's laugh.

"My instruments," he said.

I couldn't comprehend what I was feeling, hearing, seeing. Silence seemed the only option that wouldn't further submerge my flailing sanity. My companion simply smiled and continued.

"Some of us did consider moving in here when we arrived. But then we thought that it would be better used as a kind of mausoleum. Less chance of disease spreading if we keep the dead over here. Then I had the idea of putting my studio in here, and the two ideas kind of eventually meshed together."

My continued silence told him I still didn't understand.

"Dead bodies fart. Anybody who works in a morgue will tell you that. All those pipes and organs and valves finally getting to relax after all those years tensed up." He stuck out his tongue and blew a chilling raspberry, letting it echo for a second, before continuing. "The music you're hearing is basically my recordings of gas being released from corpses. I manipulate the sounds somewhat of course . . . mostly layering them on top of each other. The last CD we sent you was a new experiment I was working on where I'm actually playing the body. I've developed a kind of stopper so I can restrict the flow of air from the body, while applying pressure to certain points. It's early days yet . . . I don't think I've even begun to scratch the surface of the potential here . . . I don't think I'm far off a rudimentary scale, though."

I still couldn't talk.

"Oh, before I forget—" He produced a CD from his coat and put it in my hand. I was in so much shock that I nearly dropped it. He actually had to close my hand around it.

"The giraffe died last week . . . marvelous, elongated movements . . . this is just a rough demo of the stuff I've done with it . . . let me know what you think."

Evidently I was too stunned to ask any more questions, so we both made for the exit in silence. We cut through the shantytown and, at the bottom of the hill where it all began, he bade me farewell.

"Don't forget why we do this," he said. "Be sure and let everyone know about us."

I managed to force out a 'yes,' and scaled the hill, feeling the force of an electric current through my hair as I passed the monument. Only when I was back on North Circular Road did I begin to feel anything

like myself again. I was stunned, jaded, but also excited; my hands clutched the CD so hard it hurt, gripping to the only evidence of the strange things I'd seen that night.

I ran the short distance back to my house and slammed the door behind me. Taking the CD from its cover I placed it in the stereo and sat back in my favourite chair. As the beautiful dread of what will probably become *Ambient Morgue Volume Five* swelled and drifted through the room, I took out the photograph. It was the first one Sean had appeared in himself. He looks like some strange kind of wizard as he works away at the giraffe, like he's trying to give it back its life—reanimate it. In a way I suppose he is. It looks primitive and futuristic all at once. Slowly the magnitude of this thing started to hit me. I thought of how inspiring and revolutionary the music I was hearing was. The fact that I now knew the circumstances and conditions under which it was recorded made it all the more fantastic. After the music finished I pressed PLAY again and put it on repeat. I sat at the computer and began typing this article. What started out as a simple opinion piece about underground music gradually turned into the pocket odyssey you've just read. At this point I couldn't care less if my sanity is in question; just please, track down this morbidly angry music for yourself. It's simply some of the best sound you will hear this decade, lovingly crafted by someone that the world chose to forget, whose time to appear from the shadows seems to have arrived. ☉

Richard Howard is a speculative fiction writer from Dublin, Ireland. To date he has had stories published in *Electric Velocipede*, *M-Brane* and *Loki's Journal*. In 2008 he won the *Weird Tales* Spam Fiction contest for his story "Let Yourself Look Spiny." He currently resides in Dublin 7 where he writes, studies English, and meditates on the exact moment the humdrum becomes the fantas-

Everybody Is Waiting for Something

BY ANDREA KNEELAND

ILLUSTRATION BY STEVEN ARCHER

IN WHICH IT IS
OF STRANGE
THINGS THAT
CATACLYSMS
ARE MADE

WHEN FISH STARTED falling from the sky, Karen just shut herself up in the house with her family, hunched on the couch, waiting for some sign of reception from the television. Her husband, always the extremist, killed himself within the first twenty-four hours. Three days later, her eldest daughter, Rosalie, ran off to the Baptist church down the road, although Karen had expressly forbidden her to do anything of the sort.

Rosalie came home an hour later: the church was packed so tight with sweaty flesh that dozens of people had already lost their lives in the throes of ecclesiastical ecstasy. The causes of death were numerous: suffocation; trampling; dehydration; hyperventilation. Still, the masses inside the church were unfazed, convulsing on top of the fallen bodies in desperate prayer, speaking in tongues. The line of new converts wrapped up the church steps and around the block, hundreds of people wallowing through the thick slush of iridescent scales and reddish guts,

shielding themselves from the sky with trash can lids. Rosalie told this to her mother between bites of a ham sandwich, famished from her rebellion.

* * *

WITHIN A YEAR, life had returned to normal, as much as could be expected. Churches emptied out. Suicide rates dropped. People became embarrassed of their overreactions. Karen, for example, pretended that her hus-band had disappeared during a particularly intense fish storm; refused to admit his folly.

Karen's life had become microscopic, settled into a radius of three miles, the farthest she could walk without becoming sick from the smell of fish. Cars, airplanes, trains—any standard method of escape had become useless beneath the onslaught. She learned to predict what would be for supper that night. Thunder always indicated shellfish. Tiny clouds of gauzy cumulous suggested a smattering of shrimp. Dark autocumulous, lumpy as new black wool, foreshadowed mackerel. Everyone she knew quit their jobs (if there was any job left to quit) and settled into their respective routines: waiting for some miracle of technology to bring their television reception back, waiting for the water to finally run out beneath the absence of rainfall, waiting for the rats to get tired of rotting fish and come after the infants instead.

This, you see, was the new life. *The new life*, Karen thought, *is a tiny little thing.* She never discussed this sentiment with her daughter or her neighbors, but she knew that they agreed: the core of her bones told her so. She set a bucket out on her back porch and retired to a lawn chair beneath the eaves of the house, waiting for her dinner to fall from the sky.

IT WAS JIM Rourke who surprised everyone. Inventing a way to extract water from fish; to separate that liquid as precious as gold from the salty guts and flesh. The news was spread the old fashioned way, through gossip; through leaflets stapled to obsolete telephone poles; through a murmur of electricity, of agitation, that permeated the air.

Karen believed she remembered the name "Jim Rourke." The letters, the vowels, the composite of the alphabet spilled just that way, sparked a distant memory in her; she would have called it "nostalgia" if she hadn't already worn out the meaning of that word. She wandered about in a daze for weeks, waiting for her body to spark into excitement, the words "Jim Rourke" escaping her lips haphazardly, an accidental mantra. Finally, she pulled her yearbook from the attic and found his picture, two rows down and to the left of her own. His face, as blank and as indistinguishable as the rest of them.

The next day, she found an announcement flour-pasted to one of the telephone poles. The black lines above hung like old rubber snakes, broken and useless. She eased into her lawn chair, watching the dinner bucket, and thought about Jim's year-book portrait, about what had to become of the world before a person like him could ever be a hero.

KAREN SAT IN the town hall demonstration, swaddled fast between rows upon rows of collapsible metal chairs and sweaty flesh, her tennis shoes rubbing nervously against the high school's sticky gymnasium floor. Everybody was waiting for something to happen. She craned her head behind her shoulder, eyed the plain white clock that hung just above the closed double doors. Her head realigned itself with the front of her body and her eyes swam to the man in the front of the room. He moved toward the machine.

She watched the fish disappear inside a small box of metal, watched Jim turn the outer dial; the sputtering spigot, the tiny drops of pure, clear water running out into the little glass bowl. This water: this unbearable possibility of life.

When Karen heard the gunshot, she felt her insides shudder with queer relief; with a vague empathy for the assassin. Jim slumped across the stage, his arms flapping like the fins of a fish, blood leaking out from his heart like a faucet. The second bullet sliced clean through Jim's contraption. Glistening shards of metal and trout swam above the stage in a violent rainbow.

Karen squeezed her eyes shut. In the distance, just beyond the screams and clattering of chairs and the deafening tick of the clock, she could hear trout slapping against the roof of the building. ℮

Andrea Kneeland has no plans for the future. Her work has appeared or is forthcoming in a number of journals, including *Quick Fiction, Storyglossia, Caketrain, American Letters & Commentary, 580 Split, Night Train, elimae, DIAGRAM, alice blue review, Whiskey Island, Dogzplot* and *Lamination Colony.* Her first collection of flash fiction, *Damage Control,* is forthcoming from Paper Hero Press as part of the Fox Force 5 chapbook collective. She is also a web editor for Hobart.

P & Co.

AS YOUR SERPENT MUST EXIST ON MULTIPLE PLANES SIMULTANEOUSLY, NO MODERN CASE CAN CONFINE THEM.

"When I set upon the creation of inventory for a thousand unique items, I was certain a thing of flesh and blood would come looking for a place in it too."

A CUSTOM BLENDING OF BULL SPIRIT / EAGLE SPIRIT

AXONOMETRIC Wonder Snakes

PAGAN WICKER CARRIER

ALL SERPENTS ARE IN STOCK AND AVAILABLE TO YOU UNLESS THEY ARE NOT THOUGH THEY SHOULD STILL BE IN STOCK HERE

SUSPICIOUSLY TONGUELESS FREQUENTLY INTANGIBLE...

HISTORIC PICTISH STONES/ CURIOUS ANCIENT ART

TREE OF LIFE GIVES BIRTH TO A COLONY OF SNAKES

CAN YOU FIND THEM?

SNAKE'S WORD IS GOSPEL

MAN'S WORD IS FALSITY

HARVEY AND HIS SNAKES IN EPIMENIDES PARADOX

ORDINARY HANDLING GLOVES
COMPATIBLE WITH ALL OBJECTS‡
‡except our snakes

SS STARTER KIT easy.

1: QUART of DRIED MILK

2: HALF POUND of DRIED FRUIT
...TO BE USED WITH HANDLING GLOVES

3: VIPER SPIT - CHARM / POTION

*: ACTIVE INGREDIENT: "SOLIDIFYING" YEAST

The Buzzard

BY ERIC RED

ILLUSTRATION BY PETRAFLER

IN WHICH WE
GAIN A NEW
PERSPECTIVE ON
INTERSPECIES
RELATIONSHIPS

THE SHADOW OF the buzzard circling overhead fell over the cowboy's hat, horse and saddle soaked with blood from the hole in his belly. He slumped in his stirrups. All around, the brutal Arizona desert faded into watery waves of heat. His gun was empty. He was out of bullets and almost out of blood. The vulture knew. It had been tailing him for hours. Just that one stupid bird. Waiting for him to die. Reminding him he would soon be dead. Real soon. His bloodshot eyes glared up at the ugly carrion bird, slowly circling. The man's parched lips twisted in a defiant sneer. "Damn you, bird, you ain't gonna get me!" The vulture didn't answer, just circled. Then it disappeared from view. God, his stomach hurt. The cowboy looked around. Only endless desert badlands, scorching white sun and pounding oven heat. At least the bird was gone. He felt he had a chance again.

Just then the vulture struck with beating of huge, fetid wings that stunk of decay in the flapping wind as the bird swooped down and ripped a piece out of his shoulder. The cowboy hollered and punched blindly at the buzzard, his fingers sinking into the mottled rubbery flesh of its scrawny neck. "Oh you miserable varmint!" He shrieked. The vulture flew away with a caw of victory, a scrap of him in its cracked beak. The struggle pitched the cowboy out of his saddle and when he hit the hard ground the searing agony from the bullet in his belly sent his screams echoing across the horizon. The man lay in the dirt catching his breath. High above, the vulture circled in its grim circumference of death.

It was mocking him. The damn bird was mocking him.

The cowboy swore he would kill it before it ate him. His whole life on the range came down to one single-minded goal; to survive long enough to kill this buzzard. He hated it more than any man he had ever killed, and he had killed plenty.

He'd gotten the draw on those two rustlers who'd ambushed him at the creek and dropped them before the one got off that lucky shot that punched like a fist into his intestines. The cowboy managed to crawl back into his saddle and ride off, but had used up his ammo during the gunfight. His horse had trod down the stream for a half-mile, its hooves treading through water bright with the blood of the two dead men upstream.

That was this morning. Now he lay on the ground, mortally wounded, blinking up into the sun and the black wingspan circling above him. All he had to do was get back on his horse, he told himself. The tired nag he fell off when the buzzard attacked stood but a few yards away, head slunk in the heat. The cowboy had to get to his feet. He stumbled upright in appalling pain, warm wetness from his gut wound gushing down his leather chaps onto his boots soaked with gore and sand. He staggered in a figure eight to his saddle and got there just as the horse took off, but he had a good grip on the bridle and, cussing and screaming, he dragged and slumped himself back on the mount.

The cowboy rode again.

The vulture still circled.

The man gave it the stink eye, keeping the buzzard in sight so it couldn't ambush him anymore. The carrion bird had been flying directly overhead as the sun rose, but now it circled at one o'clock, just out of the way from blocking the burning sun so he had to stare straight into the fiery orb to spot the bird. He couldn't do it for more than a second without looking away else he would go blind, so he had to take his eye off the vulture again and again. The buzzard knew that. It was flying near the sun on purpose so it could swoop down from the sky and attack him bleeding to death on his exhausted horse. That is what vultures did. They waited out their dying prey before the feast.

He still had some life left. The cowboy figured it was a two-day ride to Yuma. The town was due west. He could make it. In town, there would be doctors and medical supplies and they'd get the bullet out of him. There would be the bite and warmth of good whisky, the smooth touch of a woman's skin, the fragrant smell of her hair, and the clean sheets after a cool bath with the gentle water against his skin. For a few precious moments, his senses strengthened with anticipation of those simple pleasures of life.

Then his horse's hoof loudly shattered a bleached dry grinning cow skull in the dirt. It was a sound like breaking pottery that grimly reminding the cowboy of his dire situation and how his time was running out. Above, the vulture cawed, like a death rattle. "I'm still here, bird, you hear me? " The man laughed manically but he felt no humor, only doom. "You ain't gonna beat me, you ugly buzzard, nossir! I'll live long enough to spit on your grave!"

The cowboy wondered what made him hate this bird so much. It was just another mangy buzzard. He's used them for target practice. But this vulture was different. It was playing a game with him. Toying with him. The cowboy had been in six gunfights and never been shot until today, and while the pain was bad, the sickening fear that his luck had run out was worse. He could die. He was dying. The bird kept reminding him of that fact; a feathered harbinger of doom that tracked him with the inescapability of death. That, or maybe he was just paranoid from loss of blood. Either way, he would kill it before it killed him. No way the cowboy was going to let the revolting scavenger eat him. "Damn you, bird, you ain't gonna get me!" He rasped through a raw parched throat.

The bird cawed as if in answer.

The cowboy pulled a bottle of rotgut whisky from his chaps and bit the cork out. He took a deep swig and felt the rank liquor numb his system. It helped a little. Seeing he had less than half a bottle left, he figured he better save it, so put the cork back in and pocketed the bottle.

And on they rode, man and bird, until sunset.

AT DUSK HE made camp.

Tying off the horse in a small arroyo, the cowboy managed to build a fire before darkness fell. As the sun dropped like a red knife slash below the horizon, he spotted the circling vulture swallowed into the gathering gloom. Then it was just night and moon and glow of fire. As painfully hot as the desert was during the day, it was just as painfully cold at night, and he shivered for warmth under his blanket. He lay with his head against a log in the glimmering glow of the campfire perimeter, staring into the flames, hypnotized by the fire licks and dancing sparks, and his thoughts wandered.

The cowboy was not a religious man. He wondered if he would go to Hell. The fire made him think of Hell, if there was a Hell. Was he a bad man? He didn't know. No worse than most, he supposed. He flashed back on his early years roping cattle and breaking horses on ranches and spreads throughout Wyoming and Idaho. He should have married his sweetheart who was pretty and loved him and he could have been in her arms right now in a warm bed

with a roof over his head rather than cold and alone and close to death out here in the desert. He wondered why left her and then he remembered. He'd left because those cattlemen had beat him up and he'd ridden off to settle the score with them. When he'd found them in a corral in the next state, he had purchased his first Remington Peacemaker and drew first and they died in the dirt. It was his way; he had to get even, when he would have been better off just turning the other cheek. The cowboy realized he was looking back on his life. Isn't that what dying men did? He wanted to live, he knew that. The cowboy would change his ways. If got out of this, when he healed up, he'd ride back to Idaho and find his sweetheart. And never leave.

The man was so tired. He couldn't keep his eyes open. He couldn't see the bird but he sure felt it. Near. Waiting for him to sleep, to lower his guard. Yeah, it was out there, alright. The fire crackled and popped, showering sparks. So tired. If only he could shut his eyes for a few minutes. No, he told himself. That was what the bird wanted. He rubbed dirt in his eyes to stay awake. It hurt like hell, and five minutes later his eyelids were drooping again. He stuck his fingers in his festering belly wound. His screams echoed across the plains. Ten minutes later sleep overcame pain and he was nodding again. He pulled out his bottle of whisky and took a long pull. The horse stood tethered to a small dead tree that looked like a stripped bone, a weary shape standing in the shadows at the edge of the meager firelight.

The cowboy heard wings. Then the sound of something landing in the darkened perimeter of the camp. His fist closed tightly on a thick, heavy branch of wood in the sand beside him. Gripping it like a club, the man carefully eased himself on his side, hugging the branch to him. He closed his eyes to narrow slits, adrenaline pumping and waking his senses. He pretended to sleep, made a snoring sound, not moving a muscle, and

watched through slitted eyelids the impenetrable gloom at the edge of the campfire.

He smelled it before he saw it.

It took a long time for the vulture to appear.

But it did. Bigger than he thought it was. A giant, hulking black feathered stinking creature with a hideous disfigured and scarred rotten red face and globular yellow eyes, its hairy jagged beak cracked and razor sharp. A death bird. Death itself.

The buzzard approached him one step at a time on huge talons waddling across the sand.

Firelight gleamed demonically in its eyes.

The bird came on slowly, step by step, watching him all the time.

The cowboy feigned slumber, completely motionless, waiting until his nemesis got within reach.

It was a foot away, silhouetted in the dying firelight.

With a caw, it pecked his hand.

And the cowboy struck.

Swinging the wooden branch in both hands with all his might against the vulture's body and head, he felt bones and cartilage crack. The buzzard shrieked in a horrible high-pitched squealing agony, eyes bulging in terror and betrayal and alarm. The man hit it again and again with the branch, trying to beat it to death. Sand and dirt flew as the bird flapped its wings violently, unable to get up or get away. Its beak gaped and a grisly tongue jutted as it cawed and yelped. The horse reared in fear, pawing the air with its hooves. The cowboy was possessed with mania as he got to his knees and brutally beat the bird, hearing its body shatter as he was splattered with its blood. The pummeled buzzard met his gaze with a feral, primal hatred that matched his own. The horse was in a panic as it jumped and whinnied, straining against its bridle and reins tethering it to the tree. Suddenly, the vulture sheared its talon savagely across his wound and the cowboy fell back, howling.

Then the bird was gone.

The man lay on the ground, curled up in pain, listening to the fading flap of wings into the sky and the wounded buzzard's cries of hurt.

He'd all but killed the thing

It wasn't coming back tonight.

THE COWBOY AWOKE with a jolt.

Daylight burned his eyes. It was morning. Shocked he had carelessly fallen asleep, the man took quick inventory of his limbs but found himself intact except for the inflamed bullet hole. Rising up painfully, he looked around the camp.

His horse lay on his side.

Dread gripped the cowboy like a nausea in his stomach. Crawling on his hands and knees, he dragged himself through the dirt to the big animal lying prone and still in the dust, saddle askew and stirrups dangling. The sound of flies became louder. The cowboy lifted his head to look over the horse's haunches, trying to spot the rising of his animal's chest with respiration. Instead, he saw the horse's blood-covered face and tongue lolling from its gaping mouth.

Its eyes had been pecked out.

With a sickening caw, the vulture leaped up. The buzzard fixed the man in a triumphant, evil, almost human gaze. It flapped its black, rotted wings and swooped up into the sky.

The bird resumed its daily circle.

The cowboy covered his head with his hands and screamed in rage, frustration and despair in the heat and the dust, pulling out hunks of his hair at the roots. "Damn you, you miserable devil, I'm gonna kill you, you dirty filthy buzzard, I'm gonna kill you if it's the last thing I do!" He staggered to his feet, unmindful of the pain of his wound, and shook his fists at the relentlessly circling vulture. It cawed loudly in response, beating its wings.

Now on foot, the cowboy headed out into the desert wastes. He knew his hour was at hand. He could make it a mile at best, before the sun was at its height and would burn like hellfire. The man knew it would be the end of him. His legs felt like cement blocks he could barely lift. His throat was raw and constricted from thirst. Delirium embraced him and white flashes flared in front of his eyes. The buzzard had won. It would eat him.

Then the cowboy had a thought. He had matches. He could drag together some brush and scrub and light it and douse himself with the last of the whisky and set himself on fire. There would be nothing left of his roasted carcass to eat and the buzzard would go away hungry. He almost did it. He had the whisky and the matches out. Then the sun began to sear his burnt skin and he realized the long pain of immolation would be an agony too great to bear. And what if he didn't die?

So the cowboy kept walking. The shadow of the vulture swept the ground ceaselessly like the second hand of a watch. His boots churned the sand. His tired eyes met the horizon. It was blurry with heat and blank and dry as a bone. He didn't want to die like this.

Far off, something metallic glinted. He stopped walking. The gleam again. When the cowboy saw the distorted figure of the man in the distance riding towards him and heard the hoof beats, he knew he wouldn't have to die today. Giving an upraised middle finger to the buzzard overhead, the man's eyes rolled up in their sockets and he passed out.

THE COWBOY SLEPT for three days the doctor told him.

When he awoke on the straw mattress in the wagon, the bullet had been removed and he had been stitched up. The kindly medical man had been in the desert collecting flowers for medicinal purposes and it had been dumb luck he had been in the right place and the right time and found the injured man suffering from loss of blood, exposure and infection. Fortunately, the doctor was skilled and saved the cowboy's life.

The cowboy expressed his gratitude and offered money, which was refused.

He accepted food and water.

He felt better.

Then he asked for the bullets.

The doctor told the cowboy that he was in no condition to go back out in the desert to settle scores.

The cowboy thanked him for everything he'd done.

He paid the doctor cash for the .45's.

By noon, he had headed out on foot into the desert, fully armed.

THE BUZZARD WASN'T hard to find.

It was just sitting there.

Like it was waiting for him.

They faced one another the way adversaries did out west.

Tumbleweed rolled.

The cowboy's hand hovered at the stock of the pistol jutting in his holster.

He fixed the vulture square in the eye.

"Draw," he chuckled, grinning.

The buzzard just watched him with its sickly yellow unblinking eyes.

The man went for his gun, grabbing the stock and sliding it out of his holster in one smooth motion with his right hand while the palm of his left hand dropped down and pressed the top of his pistol sliding it under so the quick draw movement cocked the hammer back and he pulled the trigger with the lightest touch but the gun misfired. The .45 bullet lodged in the clogged dirt in the barrel and when it exploded the whole entire pistol flew apart in jagged shrapnel in his hand.

When he regained consciousness on his back on the ground, the last thing the cowboy saw were the yellow eyes of the vulture perched on his chest, feeding and fixing him in its victorious gaze.

It wasn't about to hurry this meal. ☺

Eric Red is a motion picture screenwriter and director whose films include *The Hitcher, Near Dark, Body Parts, Bad Moon,* and the recent *100 Feet.*

The House That Smith Built

BY SIMON KING

ILLUSTRATION BY MIRMA

IN WHICH OUR
IMPULSES WILL
NOT BE DENIED,
EVEN IF PERHAPS
THEY SHOULD BE

TIME IS SHORT; so forgive me if I censure those images I deem gratuitous and fat. Walk with me instead. Fog will surround us, hiding our vision of some things, but we will see others. Right now all you need to see is me. If you feel grass, wet with dew, fold beneath your feet, then that is your business not mine.

From up ahead, where the fog thins, come the sounds of rhythmic bangs and screams. Note these. Also, try to note the broken bricks upon the ground that have fallen from the house beyond. Try to see through the fog so that you can picture its broken walls, and the timber supports of a roof, that, having committed adultery, has divorced and left.

It is to this broken house that we head.

Having reached the house, I suggest that you note the doorway. It is crumbling fast, but the name 'Smith' still stands above it. The name may be important to you, but we must move on. So please, follow me into the house for a moment. You may notice, if you are so inclined, that grass covers the floor here too, and that any partitions within the house have long since gone.

The bangs are near their strongest here, and if we turn our heads we may locate their source.

The erect and rusted barrel of an old man's rifle. Paint for him whatever portrait your mind desires for he is shrouded in fog; only remember that he is old. Remember too that in his hands, perpendicular to his body, he grips a rifle. His rifle he fires down the length of the house, and each expulsion of sound is followed by a scream.

Suppose for an instant that this collocation of sound has not forced us to flee, and that instead we move to the other end of the house to investigate. Suppose that we see a corpse hanging from the rafters there. For the most part the corpse is a pulpish mash that swings with each fresh shot. This is the body of a younger man. Its face, the only part of its body free of wounds, is but a younger imitation of the old man, only starved of air, with a fatted purpled tongue hanging slack from its mouth. Arrange the facial details as you will, just ensure that it is dead and unable to emit the shredding screams. Attribute these to the woman by his feet.

She clings to the stumps of his legs, down where the fog is thickest. This woman, she is both young and beautiful, and since the fog is too thick for you to see her, and since her beauty will distract too much in describing, assign to her what aesthetic qualities you will; free me time to leave her for a while, for one last person remains. She stands by the old man's side and watches.

She is old, and her face, weary of standing above her shoulders, has dropped into her chest. Hair-covered knees ball beneath a faded floral dress. If you feel it is necessary to be repulsed you may, but stay by my side for a while longer at least. She has a story to tell.

The old man is her husband; it is they who are named Smith.

They were still happily married when they were old, and they lived within the house that we stand in now; though in those old days it was in better repair, for the man worked to keep it so. But then the woman, the woman who now screams came.

She was young, and she was beautiful, and she came from nowhere. She lived in the fields surrounding the house, for there was no one and nothing around, and everyday she would talk to the old man as he worked on the house, but the old woman was not afraid. The man's desires for sex and such things that are related had died at the end of his youth.

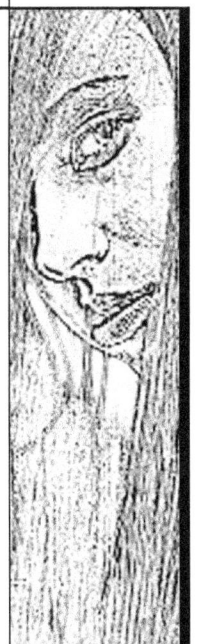

Over time however, and over the days that passed, he began to spend longer and longer with the young woman. He would go off into the fields with her for hours on end, forget about the house. And so, brick by brick, the house began to fall.

One day the old woman went out into the fields, and found her husband lying with the young woman. When the old man, out of shame and formality arose, he found that where he had lain the young woman had birthed him a son, the image of himself at twenty.

The old man and the old woman stood there, and as they stood there the old man's son lay with the young woman, again and again, and as he did so the house crumbled further. The old man watched, until, unable to watch anymore, he seized his son; and from the rafters of his house hanged him.

After the hanging the young woman clung to the son's legs, and after a time his heart's slow beat returned. It was then that the old man took up the gun, and, rifle erect, fired at his son, so that the woman could not return him to life. But after it was done, and the sobbing continued, the heartbeat came again, followed by a bullet.

But the old woman knows her husband cannot fire forever. One day his bullets will run out, and when he can no longer fire, then the young woman will return his son to life, and she will lie with him again, and the house will crumble once more.

Listen now, the banging has stopped; another brick falls. ☯

Simon King is from that part of North England where mammoths still roam and grumpy dragons claim for free bus passes. He isn't from that part where people shout 'You lookin' at my woman', and he doesn't think that people actually do that. In his free time he studies creative writing at Kingston University, tidies the magazines at W.H. Smiths, and gets very, very close to finishing a novel about seaside towns, dangerous obsessions, fires in London and Marlene Dietrich brought back from the

The Men in That Water

BY ZDRAVKA EVTIMOVA

ILLUSTRATION BY STEVEN ARCHER

IN WHICH A WOMAN, A MAN, AND AN EDIBLE ASTEROID SEEK AN ARRANGEMENT

I DIDN'T FORCE them. They did it of their own accord. They dipped their fingers into the transparent jar full water and the water took them. It dissolved them. I didn't have any strategy, I made no plans. I didn't lie to the men the way you'd expect. I didn't ask after their names. I was generous, I wasted my time on them, I took them to the ocean, that endless huge mass that had no beginning and no end.

The man himself chose the jar in which he'd be dissolved. Most of them were vain. They chose their jars for hours and often returned to change it. They paid for fancy jars with gold bands and red luminescent hearts engraved on the glass.

I didn't feel anything, no guilt, no pangs of remorse. When the guy dipped his finger in the jar he was no more. The water dissolved him and remained transparent, pure and quiet in its clean vessel. I often wondered what happened to the men in that water. The advertisement said it was very easy to transport human beings dissolved in the water from the ocean to other places where tungsten extraction throve. Maybe there the experts put them together again. I didn't know how they did that,

I guessed they did something to the water I'd taken from the ocean, and then the men were alive and kicking again, ready to toil away in the tungsten mines.

I often wondered what would happen if you drank the water in which a man had dissolved. I wouldn't do that. I wouldn't honestly.

Drugan was a quiet asteroid where nothing happened. One tenth part of it was land, perfectly flat, always the same serene green color. At some places the land tasted like smoked cheese, at others it reminded you of chocolate and maple syrup. When I wandered the Asteroid far and wide, I discovered many different tastes, which I couldn't compare to the foods I'd tasted back on the earth. Maybe I should have waited for the scientists to make their analyses and tell me if the land of the Asteroid was poisonous. Well, scientists were a tardy and oppressively slow lot, and back then I didn't have money. I didn't have health insurance either and I had borrowed money from all friends, relatives and acquaintances whose names still had not slipped out of my memory, and the Asteroid was a blessing in disguise for me. The first time I had eaten from its land I expected I'd be dead within hours, but I wasn't. The Asteroid's land tasted of apples and I stayed grateful to that quiet nook I had discovered by chance. Then I moved south, to the ocean, and the land changed. Now it tasted like chips. The sky was red all the time, deep strong red. There was no wind and there was no rain, no snow, just the endless land you could eat. I didn't need water. I ate the land and I was never thirsty, it was as simple as that. All the information the tourist brochures offered was, "Don't drink from the ocean. The ocean is deathly dangerous." Then I met a woman. She was lying on the smooth blue land.

"I have no money," she said. "I've been living on the Asteroid for two eons now."

I didn't know anything about the eons back then.

"Two eons?" I gasped. "What does that mean?"

She smiled and I loved her smile.

"Who's thrown you here at the back of beyond?" she asked. I told her I didn't have money and I didn't have water to drink.

"Go south then," she said. "The land there tastes like water and it quenches your thirst."

"Where's south?" I asked. There was no way to know, there were no stars on the red sky, and there were no days and no nights, just bright warm light like a blanket over the blue land.

"South is the ocean." She said. Then I was suddenly aware I didn't know her name.

"What's your name?"

"Ocea," she said. "I chose my name after the Ocean."

She's crazy, I thought. Only idiots and scumbags like me stayed on the Asteroid. Yes, it was cheap – you didn't pay rent, you didn't go to supermarkets. You mooned around a place eons and eons on end, and ate the land of the Asteroid. Sometimes, when I went searching for land of a different taste, I chanced upon small gangs of guys. They were very fat and they lay prostrate, eating the land. They stuck their mouths to shallow holes they had dug as they guzzled the blue delicious soil. Most of the men I had seen didn't have clothes on. I noticed only old torn rags on them.

"Have you met him?" the woman asked quietly squinting at me.

"Met whom?" At first, I thought she had in mind one of the hobos who loafed about the shore, eating big hollows into the land in which later he slept.

"The advertisement man," she said staring at me intently.

"Who's the advertisement man?" I asked.

"He's the man who buys jars of water," she said. "He's been after me almost two eons."

"What's an eon?" I again asked her.

"Eon is the time after which the taste of the land changes."

"What!"

"The first eon I was on the Asteroid the land was cold and salty almost everywhere. Then suddenly it was good to eat. I started eating it. But the ocean…"

"What about the ocean?" I asked.

"I don't know," she said. "I'm afraid to go near it."

"Why?" I asked.

The ocean was flat and perfectly calm. It was crystal clear, pure and transparent. It never moved. It didn't produce any sounds it emitted no heat, and exuded no smell. It was endless, enormous, and boundless under the red sky, and it touched the blue land without stirring the smallest grain of sand. Several times I had thrown pieces of blue soil into it, expecting a miracle. Nothing happened. The water took the blue chunks and they vanished. I threw into it my only rusty iron saucer I had brought with me from the Earth. I didn't need it. I could eat as I lay on the flat blue surface of Drugan. The ocean gulped down my saucer and made no noise. In the beginning, I used a knife to cut and carve pieces from the blue soil, then I saw knives made no sense here. I could easily bite off lumps of the land. It was a queer place, that Asteroid. Just a speck on the space map and a tiny paragraph: "Asteroid Drugan: Cheap Living, Favorable Climatic Conditions. Avoid contact with the ocean. It is assumed it might be dangerous. Chemical composition of the land is still insufficiently explored." And it would remain unexplored, of course. The first expedition discovered no tungsten ore. There were heavy odds against scientists poking their clever noses in the water.

I looked at the woman. What was she doing here? She was pretty, but of course all women were pretty. Their parents should be very poor indeed if they couldn't afford some shabby expert in genetics to engineer a beautiful daughter for them. I'd rather have a plain woman. Thus I was convinced the features of her face would remain stable.

You never knew when something would go wrong and the beauty the quack doctors had produced would turn into a heap of wrinkles and disheveled patches of withered skin.

"You are beautiful, Ocea," I told her all the same.

"I guess this is no longer a compliment, but I'd rather accept it as one," she said and smiled again. Her eyes were deep blue like the ground, and her brown hair appeared copper and russet in the red iridescence of the sky.

"THE ADVERTISEMENT MAN comes once every eon," she said. I didn't know if an eon was a long time.

"What does he want?"

"He wants water," she mumbled.

"There's so much water in the ocean," I pointed out. I had never approached the ocean although it seemed quiet and friendly. I had watched it till my eyes hurt. It was perfectly still as if it had frozen long time ago. It was transparent, bottomless and immobile.

"You don't understand," she said. "The advertisement man pays for the ocean with a man dissolved in it."

"Why?"

She didn't answer. Her face was smooth and clean, and I wondered how long it would keep on like that. I'd seen beautiful women whose faces disintegrated before my eyes, turning into a mashed mess of blood and shriveled skin. The parents most probably had hired a cheap doctor to model a beautiful baby for them. But cheap was always cheap and the face of the girl lasted for a couple of years. The gene transformers the doctor had used were cheap and the face ended up cheap in the long run. The women I knew back on the earth wanted to have sex before their faces disintegrated. I wondered how long Ocea's face would hold on beautiful and whole.

"How much does the advertisement man pay for a jar?" I asked.

"Don't even think about it!" she snarled baring her teeth. That surprised me.

Women I knew never did like that. Snarling would make their faces fall apart almost instantly. Was it possible she was not genetically engineered? Her skin was smooth, her lips were full and there was not a single defect to her face. It was unthinkable for a normal woman to be that perfect.

"Don't even think about what?" I asked.

"Many have tried before you," she snarled once again, her cheeks twisting and twitching.

"Tried what!" I shouted. I hated it when a woman pulled a wry face at me, engineered or real.

"They tried to dip my fingers into a jar," she suddenly said looking me in the eye.

"What happened after that?" I was intrigued.

"I won't tell you," she glared at me. "Go to the south and see for yourself."

"What is there to see?" I asked trying to calm down.

"Nothing to see and a lot to hear," she said still glowering at me. "You can hear them moan."

'Why?'

There was a long heavy silence, in which her thin body jutted out like dust devil, slowly sailing away in the distance. The asteroid was quiet; its blue land, flat, unobtrusive, spread as far as the eye could see. I was sure it was delicious if you could bite a chunk off it.

"Listen!" she hissed. "Can't you hear them?"

I could. I heard muffled voices, thick and hoarse, pushing their way deep into the land. I couldn't discern any words, the voices were so jumbled. They hit and jostled each other, they rumbled like a waterfall buried under ocean.

"What's that?" I asked.

"Do you know the holes with the ragged sluggards wallowing in them? The fat guys, who lie and eat all the time."

"Yes, I've seen some of those," I said.

"A couple of them tried to dip me into the jar of the advertisement man," she said

defiantly. "Well, I dipped their hands into that jar."

"So what?" I muttered.

"They dissolved," she said. "All of them . . . They were asleep when I dipped their fingers into the water. But I didn't sell anything to the man."

I looked at her. Her dark blue eyes told me nothing. They burned and sparkled dangerously.

"I didn't sell the jar." She repeated. "I poured it out there," she pointed to the dark blue patch of land that groaned and screeched with the muffled power of angry men's voices. I stared.

'There are so many big fat men sleeping in their holes," she repeated. "They've gobbled up much of the land."

"What's wrong with that?"

Now she stared at me. I knew the ocean was quite far from here and I asked myself where those muffled men's voices came from.

"The water, which has dissolved somebody, is odd," she said. "If you spill it onto the sand, the land starts speaking." At that point I was sure she was off her rocker. I watched her face closely. Her forehead appeared purple with the crimson light flooding from the sky, and her chin was blue like the land that babbled in the voices of the missing men. "But that talking land is no good," she went on slowly. "It . . . it tells you things. It's creepy . . . "

"Creepy?" I repeated looking at her.

"Go ahead and eat from it," she said then suddenly dashed away from me, away from the land that spoke in the voices of the men who were no more. She ran noiselessly like a flame of a torch, like a light from a star, her figure gradually turning red, mingling with the crimson immensity of the sky.

I wondered why she had run away. Her feet had left no trails on the hard blue ground. Soon there was nothing of her, and I asked myself I had not imagined it all.

I saw strange things on the Asteroid. I learned that if you ate from the soil near the ocean you had queer dreams. You dreamt about the time when you were a kid and your mother was there holding your hand, teaching you to ride a bicycle. I came to know that if you took a bite out of the softer land near the shore you suddenly hated the red sky. You howled at it and spat at it, but it was there all the same, big and thick sky, which glared purple and wild at you. All the time, the jumble of voices sounded stronger and I thought – what the hell. I went to the hollows in which the fat guys lay, chewing the blue slabs of soil, thrusting into their mouths sand and blue clayey mud, their lips frothing or bleeding. I cut off a small chunk from that land and put a piece of it in my mouth. There was nothing particular about the taste. It resembled white feta cheese I disliked from an early age. Then the wild thing happened. My body tingled pleasantly, my limbs felt blissfully hot and a sensation of pleasure filled me, every inch of my skin, every cell in my body. My blood and my bones throbbed happily. My brain whirled and glittered with the feeling of indescribable satisfaction. All the time the blind heavy jumble of voices sounded in my ears and I swam there, amidst the voices, my body thrilled and gratified. It felt like having the most magnificent, the most savage and glorious sex. I didn't want it to end. I dug my nails into the blue ground nibbling at it, champing it, chewing it, choking on it. I wanted more. I wanted to swallow the voices in the blue soil. I wanted to devour them. I could gobble the whole asteroid.

"Hey, hey! Stop!" somebody was spanking me, pulling me away from the unbelievable blue avalanche of bliss.

"You've got enough! Stop it!" a voice shouted. It was a voice I vaguely remembered. I couldn't see anything but the delicious dollops I had wrenched from the blue land. I wanted them in my mouth, in my throat, in by belly. I'd die for them.

"The Asteroid will suffocate you. Stop!"

Then I saw her. The woman was trying to drag me way from the chanting moaning soil. No, you idiot, leave me alone! I saw her hitting me on the head with her heel.

"Now you know what that the ocean does when you dissolve somebody in it," she whispered ready to plant her heel in my neck again. "Look at them!"

I saw the guys in their deep holes, which they had bitten and gnawed in the blue hard soil. They were fat, sniggering, drooling, their faces all covered with blue dust. Around them, the jumble of voices buzzed, droned and whirred.

"Now you know why the advertisement man buys those jars," she said. "Now you know why the blue land speaks."

I looked at her. She bent over me, tall, thin, her dark blue eyes telling me nothing, half of her face red like the sky, the other purple like the immensity of the land.

"Will you dip my finger into a jar?" I whispered.

"No" she said bending down.

Then she kissed me.

"One is lonely on the Asteroid," she whispered.

Love felt lonely and magnificent. She was more than love could give me. She was the infinite land, the tortured sky and the dead ocean. The whisper of the vanishing men was in her. It was in me too, I was the Asteroid, I was the ocean, and I loved her the way the land loved the men who devoured it. She was the sand in the holes of the moaning men, and she was their digging teeth. I loved her the way I loved the wind that was never there but I dreamt of it. I loved her like I loved my memories of the earth.

"Ivan" she said. I thought she'd say she loved me. All the women I knew did that. Love was easy all the time, you simply bought a LGD, Love Generating Device, and it sent your brain its rays. You'd love anybody that you stumbled upon a minute after the rays of LGD worked on you. Then you

forgot and it was all right. You paid for another LGD and you loved again. The women told you that you were their dream come true, even if the LGD had been a really cheap one.

"I KNOW I'M everything for you," he said. Now her face was small, a tiny white patch against the blue land.

"You'll dip my finger into a jar and you'll sell me," she said

It was quiet and he didn't mind her babbling. He asked himself how much a jar with a man in it cost. He didn't know.

"I dreamed about you before I met you," she went on. "I dreamed you dipped my finger into the ocean. You got rich . . . You met the advertisement man."

He loved her. The Asteroid was in his blood when he touched her, and it was magnificent.

"You are everything beautiful I've lived through," she whispered.

"Shut up," he said. Love happened so pleasantly with her. He liked her face. He loved her honestly. With her it felt even better than after he'd paid for the LGD. No one of his acquaintances on the earth would believe it was possible. He couldn't believe it. He asked himself if all this was not another idiotic dream.

"I know you'll sell me," she said. "I know you'd be rich. But . . . "

He wouldn't let her babble on. He knew that love was a temporary sensation. It would be over and he'd be alone in the blue wilderness of quiet and peace. He'd be alone with the rustling sounds, the ones the fat guys produced while they chewed the blue land and transformed it into bliss. He had great plans. He'd be somebody. He'd be a man to be reckoned with.

. . . He had no strategy, no cunning plans. He simply went to the big blue holes in which the fat man lived. They bit off blue pieces of the land, they masticated and digested it, enveloped by abominable stink, by thick blue vapors, their faces smiling, their

bodies swollen, enormous, jutting out of the trenches, the shallow pits and cavities they'd eaten into the soil.

He simply offered them the jar he had filled with the water from the endless ocean. It was not necessary to tell them anything. They were ready, sprawled out on the floor of their hollows, smelling obnoxiously. He was appalled when he touched them. He grabbed their wrists and dipped the whole hand into in the jar. Then the fat men were no more. They disappeared.

"Where have they gone?" he asked himself, not that he cared much. Not that he cared at all. He poured some of the water from the jar just to be sure the guy was in there. The blue sand started speaking right away. Sometimes he listened. The water with the guy in it told horrific stories. It told you about the guy, about his mother, that he had not still forgotten. It told you about the girls he had enjoyed. He regretted he was not a writer, he could have made a fortune if he wrote down what the guys in the water babbled. Then he simply stopped listening to them. If he unwittingly spilled the water, he ran away because the speaking sands got on his nerves. He collected dozens and dozens of jars and looked for the advertisement man. He crisscrossed the Asteroid, he went to the south, and he knew the tastes of the blue land at all latitudes. There is no advertisement man, he thought, desperate. She'd lied to me. I won't ever be rich.

He heaped the jars around him then he started building a house with them. The water was transparent, but the light of the red sky gave it a scarlet glow. There were no more guys he could dissolve in his jars. He was alone on the asteroid hoping against hope to meet the advertisement man.

"It's lonely on the Asteroid," he remembered her saying. He was lonely, yes. Every night he poured some water on the sand to drive away the blue loneliness that crept into him. He listened to the voice of the man in the jar, he listened about the man's mother, about his imaginary girlfriends and

he was scared, he was scared stiff. He remembered the wretched cavity in the sand, in which the man had lived and he remembered the stink.

"What have I done," he muttered every time he woke to the voices of the men he had offered the ocean water. He wished he could go back to the earth, but he had no money.

Then she came again. She appeared out of nowhere, her thin slim figure cut against the sky. He didn't know how to tell her how happy he was. He kissed her and he loved her happily, madly. He loved her face, he loved its red half and he loved its blue half, and he didn't care if her parents had had enough money to pay a good genetic engineer or not. He was happy she was there.

Then she suddenly pushed him. Her blue eyes told him nothing. Distant eyes that were flat like the ocean.

"I have an offer for you," she said slowly looking him in the eye. "I want to buy the jars and the guys you dissolved in them."

"What?" he couldn't believe.

"I'll pay you," she went on quietly, her hands that a minute gave him everything now away from him. "All this will be yours," she said showing him a bag. It was full of microchips which cured your diseases, brought girlfriends to you, and bought you a planet where no harmful microorganisms lived. She showed him microchips no human had seen before.

"All this will be yours," she repeated.

"Really?" he mouthed. He still couldn't believe.

"You've worked hard and you deserve it," she said. "I want you to go and sprinkle all the jars on the sands. Now!

"Are you crazy?" Ivan still couldn't believe. "The water will to go to waste. I'll lose everything!"

"How do you think all writers came to be? Can you imagine a normal human being wasting his time scribbling nonsense? They all pay dearly for a jar of speaking sand."

He stared. He saw the blue sands, the interminable flat ocean, he saw her and he knew he had been happy before, when he had only the memory of her figure, slim and gentle against the red sky.

"I had never thought the Asteroid was beautiful before I met you," he said.

"That worked," she said smiling. "Otherwise you wouldn't remain with the sluggards."

He looked at the dead beach of the immobile ocean. The water was perfectly calm. There were no waves, no ripples. He stared at the immense flat wasteland.

"Ocea!" he whispered.

She was advancing slowly on him, thrusting a jar of transparent water at his face.

"What are you doing?" he asked.

She threw the water of the jar in his eyes.

He saw the ocean rise. Its gigantic transparent columns loomed magnificent, terrible. Then enormous sounds roared and rumbled, the water was flat again, immobile, the columns died and vanished in a flash, but the sounds remained. They were strong, pure, brilliant, gorgeous. The mad ocean was singing, its song magnificent, unbelievable. You are my everything. You are my shore and my infinity. I love you, Ocea. The water was there, with him.

"Who are you?" he managed to whisper.

"I am the advertisement man," the woman answered, her forehead red with the glow of the sky, her chin blue like the sand.

No one could hear her words. ☉

Zdravka Evtimova is a Bulgarian writer and translator living in Belgium. Her short stories have been published in the USA, Great Britain, Canada, Australia, Germany, France, India, Poland, Russia, Czech Republic, Slovenia, Macedonia and Serbia in *Mississippi Review Online, Metropole, Antioch Review, New London Writers, Quality Women's Fiction,* and many others. In Bulgaria she has three short story collections and three novels. She is currently working on a novel entitled *Arrogant* and translating her novel *God of Traitors* into English.

Errata Slip Found in a Copy of the Arkham University Press Trade Paperback Reissue of the Necronomicon

{ SUBMITTED BY MICHAEL SWANWICK }

on p. 3. "Ph'nglui mglw'nafh Cthulhu R'lyeh wgah'nagl fhtagn," usually translated as "In his house at R'lyeh dead Cthulhu waits dreaming," should be cast in the future perfect continuous tense: "Ph'ngluu mglw'nafh Cthulhu R'lyeh wgah'nagl fhta'gn," indicating that our once and future dread master "shall have been [revealed to be] continuing to dream." A subtle distinction, but we've had complaints.

on pp. 241-6, the formulation for raising a djainn lacks a rite of closure. You shouldn't be dealing with Damned Beings in the first place, but if you absolutely must, it's a sine qua non that you have a closing formulary. Simply reverse the wording of the opening formulary and rephrase it as a double-negative.

on p. 317, "would be a good idea" should properly be "would not be a good idea." Trust us on this one.

Lastly, the final three pages should be immediately ripped out and burned without reading. We simply cannot emphasize this enough. Unfortunately, our compositor went mad after reading the proof sheets, as did the graduate student we hired to razor the offending passage out of individual copies. We realize that you may be tempted to read it anyway. But madness is the least you have to fear. Everybody even peripherally associated with those pages has

HOME FOR THE HOLIDAYS

BY LUCY A. SNYDER

Six months past the New Year's
car crash, I heard him from beyond
the grave: "Honey, I'll be with you
in time for Christmas." And my love

was true. Elms blushed for autumn
when his appendix arrived,
pink as Labor Day sunburn.
How our baby laughed to see it!

Then his pumpkin-fat spleen,
just in time for Halloween.
Icy Thanksgiving roads
glazed in warm vodka

served up his steady legs.
The last chilly Chanukah night
his sweet Manischewitz toast
brought the rest of him home.

Our family will share
the Yuletide snug
in our dark pine abode
beneath December snows.

Twisted

BY KEVIN VEALE

ILLUSTRATIONS BY MARC ROBINSON

IN WHICH TWO MEN EMBARK ON A DESPERATE QUEST FOR DRUGS IN THE ZOMBIE-RIDDEN HEARTLAND OF AMERICA

WE WERE DRIVING past Kalamazoo towards the edge of the desert when the withdrawal began to set in. I remember feeling light-headed for moments before phantom weevils scuttled down my spine. Caustic burblings oozed through my gut. Dogwood, my Minister for Lateral Problem-Solving, looked askance at me under his dust-encrusted ski-goggles.

"We can't stop again, man."

He left it at that, aware I understood the situation. The Minister had insisted on liberating a convertible and driving it with the top down across broken plains that required goggles to shield the eyes. Our holy mission necessitated a certain vibe, he'd argued, and felt this justified grit in the teeth and a car with a dying battery. Besides, it was all right for him: I'd been seeking gastro-intestinal regularity by varying the elements of my drug intake, producing gut-locked stony constipation on one side, and fluid Lovecraftian bowel-horrors on the other.

Our rationing was forcing me towards Accidental Soiling, and the Minister jouncing us at high speed across the dusty hills

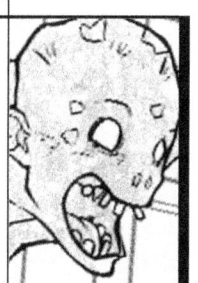

towards the yellowing bowl of Lake Michigan didn't help.

Dogwood elbowed me then—distracting me from a passing cramp—and pointed out to a ditch ahead of us. It was surrounded by clouds of flies over corpses, like the foaming head on some sun-warmed simmering flesh-beer.

Not a good place to stop, no.

Dogwood pawed one-handed at one of our satchels of Supplies as we crested a cracked rise above the sprawling incline of the desert bowl: "I need amyl nitrite. Popper. Just the one. Keep me focused."

"Our resolve must be strong, Minister," I said, thrusting forward a heroic chin.

"Screw resolve! Gimme!"

I understood the battery situation, and the Minister understood the drug situation. Then again, he'd also insisted on calling me "Horse," since he'd learned we intended to cross the desert, and did nothing but giggle when I demanded explanations. I pulled the bag out of his reach as our car picked up speed and caught sight of movement behind us in the wing-mirror. A zombie clambered out of the flesh-beer like a whale breaching in a thick sea of meat and tried to follow us down the slope. I winced and shook myself—truly, this was a bad scene. I then settled back into my seat just in time for the Minister to guide our descent into an old drier, half-sunk in crusted Michigan mud, the impact smashing us briefly airborne.

"You did that on purpose!" I cried stridently.

"An amyl would help me drive."

I remember bickering as the corpse behind us fell away in the dust, following our movement since it couldn't smell us. Dogwood eventually had his amyl, I made vile assertions about his mother, and peace was restored.

I REMEMBER THAT our mission happened the same year as the infamous Presidential debate between Ozzy Osbourne and Tommy Lee, or would have done if either of them had turned up. Perhaps nobody told them, but it had been a great party nonetheless.

Our essential problem was that our home town of Bad Axe was not a key pharmacopeia to greater Michigan, and as such the supply of drugs available to we survivors was becoming thin. The Minister and I had realized this and begun to spread the word.

It had been a clear morning when we saw Smiley Fletcher staggering down the street, haggard and horrified through the pains of withdrawal. When some of the ubiquitous zombies turned toward him in one movement and began to close in, it had all became clear. The Minister crash-tackled Smiley to the ground and held him down while I squirted wood glue—nice and toxic—into a supermarket fruit-bag, hands thick and nerveless with my own drug song. I handed it to Dogwood, who covered Smiley's face and roared "You *reckless bastard!*" as Smiley sucked down the fumes and went limp.

I remember waving vaguely—I was deep in a Green Shrieker spiral, beatific, wise and spiritually well-hung as Christ on a stump—and declaiming, "Forgive him, Minister, he knows not what he do. Does . . . ? Whatever."

The Minister had ignored me, but we each took an end of the man and hustled him away from the zombies activated by his sobriety. I took the time to waft glue fumes around to further mask the scent, and we got him to safety. There is, however, a central problem with the Emergency Glue, or Emergency Drugs as a wider class: it is very difficult to interrogate someone high as a kite.

So we'd given up.

Indeed. Ours is an interesting society.

In the days that followed, the scope of the problem became clear. Drugs, however communal, were running low in Bad Axe. All but the cheapest, nastiest gunge was gone, and it is a truly sad state of affairs when a liberated society dependant on illicit pharmaceuticals for its very survival *isn't having fun.* So the Minister and I had scrounged up our supplies along with what anyone else could be persuaded to part with, taking it upon ourselves to quest forth for the common good.

Dogwood was along as Minister for Lateral Problem-Solving due to his greater experience in escaping lock-up situations. The man kept a spare Zippo in one boot for the express purpose of starting distraction fires, and his inclusion seemed a good idea at the time. I, sterner of vision and focus, was the noble leader.

AS WE CAREENED down Lake Michigan I remember noting that the Minister's horrible hat was still on his greasy head, despite my demands he throw it away. A graying and cracked nacho cowboy hat, serrated at the rim with flaked chips, which the Minister had sprayed with lacquer weeks before as a preservative. The bell of the hat, originally filled with plastic petrochemical cheese, was crusted with dead flies and cigarette ash beneath layers of road dust.

It was an undying affront to gods and men alike. How could he possibly *not know* the hideousness of the lamentable hat? Perhaps it had been only to spite me, and had I not mentioned my Hate for the thing it would have slipped the Minister's mind and been forgotten. And yet here we were.

I refused to fill our journey with the baboon squeals and high gibbering which would follow a defense of the Hat, so bore its company in silence, hoping it would shake itself apart as Dogwood drove.

Our immediate mission was but part of a larger path that I had been travelling at the time, Minister Dogwood at my side. We were used to each other, and this helped explain what I was doing stuck in a convertible beside a man wearing a scrofulous nacho hat and filthy ski-goggles. We plummeted on bad suspension towards the damp flats of Lake Michigan, with its treacherous patches of sucking mud and sundered machine hulks like the rising rusted fists of days gone by.

* * *

NIGHT FOUND US on the far side of Lake Michigan in a scrubby wooded area, dying trees around a fire that was objectively dangerous in the dry conditions. As the Minister had said, "Screw it, it's cold."

And it was cold, night in this new pupating desert. Over-irrigation had salted the earth, which had been survivable till the Feds drained our water-table and routed it to wealthier drought-stricken parts of our fair feral nation. Once they had, the salts settled out and nothing new would grow, leaving us with a savage new landform on our doorstep, waiting to be born.

I had always wondered what it had been like for the Feds when the dead rose. All those DEA guys figuring out that their stockpiles of confiscated drugs could be the key to survival. You'd have straight-laced preppy swine taking *precise, measured doses* of whatever they had nearby to stave off the hungry dead. Which would have worked great, right until Cookie Monster lunged for them from the dark foot-well of their desk, shrieking in unhallowed tongues.

That's the thing, you see. The levels of drugs required for safety aren't the kinds of demons you can dance with and expect to get away unscathed. They're going to ride you, scar you, write their initials in your skin… and occasionally one is going to climb into your skull, grab the wheel and take you for a ride.

The Minister, myself, and those like us have enough experience to respect the demons and know that expecting to keep control is folly, leading only to Bad Craziness. Roll with the punches, embrace the demons and surrender.

The Suits? How they'd have handled it? I wish I could have seen.

Had a friend called Shanks once whose theory was that the zombies tracked brain activity, and so drugs messed you up enough that they couldn't find you.

Then again, this is from a guy who became so monstrously drunk with the technician of his local black-market Augmentation

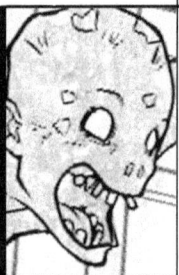

chop-shop that he wound up with a Mister Stun implant where a Mister Stud implant should go, the poor bastard. Heard he found a girl who likes that recently, though. Calls him "Tickler."

But that's beside the point.

What you need will not play nice, will not play fair, but it means you can sleep without being surrounded by groaning fiends come morning. That was how they got you. Sooner or later you have to sleep. The central benefit of our lifestyle was that when I saw the fetid corpse of my first crush reaching out to tear off my face, I could be *practically certain* it wasn't real. It made for an interesting transition period, but after a while the wandering dead fell away into background irrelevance, like parking wardens and homeless people before the world changed.

Such peace was not always two-way. I remember that our evening's ration carried the Minister away on a tide of energy and impulse-control problems. We were still clad in our road clothes, the Minister in the Lamentable Hat and a blue Hawaiian shirt decorated in dirty playing cards, with unclean jeans and army boots. Dust and silt ground into his face except for patches left by the goggles, like some demented reverse-raccoon with mania shining in bright eyes. He'd found three or so zombies lurking nearby our fire-pit, and was gleefully diving and swooping around the lumbering beasts, seeking opportunities to tie their shoelaces together and watch them shuffle and stumble about. I can't recall what I wore myself, just that it was cold so I sought my sleeping-bag early.

In retrospect this was probably for the best. Soon after that, I worked through the lag you get with decent mescaline and suddenly everything mattered less. I was still aware of the Minister gallumphing around in his untied army boots, but was rapidly distracted by drifts of red, juicy butterflies hanging from tree branches like ripe fruit. What *were* these things, I remember thinking? Thick, fleshy wings, like ham steaks,

flaps of foreskin or perhaps thickly sliced tomato, with no bodies to speak of. In a resonant conundrum, perhaps they were all of these *at the same time*. This needed more thought, I decided.

They shivered delicately with every muffled roar or clatter Dogwood produced, the motion echoing in my nervous system like they were under my skin. I understood instantly that his noise offended them, and terror that they might flee thrilled through me. I was considering how best to calm the Minister—couldn't he see how he frightened these poor things?—when a succession of sharp popping cracks, each one electricity flaring down my skull and out my limbs, filled the air and startled the hamforeskintomatoflies. Then someone screamed.

I was already on my feet before I consciously thought, *Christ, what's the Minister doing now?* And found myself heading towards the source of the noise. I located Dogwood, stripped to the waist but still wearing the Hat, wrestling with a dark woman in combat fatigues. Fallen zombies littered the ground around them, all shot in the head, but more silhouettes were grumbling towards us through the trees.

"Glue, Horse!" the Minister roared.

I hiccupped and ran back to the camp on uneven feet as bruised flesh-petals fell in slow flurries, the delicate crimson creatures in the trees coming apart from the stressful vibrations humming all around us. The wood-glue leapt into the plastic bag like an oddly warm, fat voluptuous slug, making me squeal.

How had this happened, I wondered? Confusing beauty swirled into malevolent slugs and screams in the night, leaving me bewildered and undone.

The Minister was hustling the woman towards me through the dry and dying trees in a near headlock, one arm twisted behind her back. I held the gruesome pulsating slug-bag to her face, prompting muffled screams and sharp movements as she tried to get away.

"Take it, you daft cow!" hissed the Minister, for he had grown up a Briton and was prone to slipping into the vernacular of his youth in times of crisis. "Breathe it in."

She went limp, which made it easier for us to drag her away from the pursuing zombies and the eerily silent patient tread they always fell into when following prey. I fell back, waving the glue around to confuse the trail and hoped that would lose them. The dead are dull-witted but canny predators, like some form of flesh-eating math teacher, but once they're agitated and activated by potential food, they'll go for anything in the vicinity whether it's medicated or not.

You're either good and fucked up or a danger to everyone, nothing in between. The Minister was furious. We dropped her, swooning and puking, back at the camp and wordlessly took up our weapons—a crowbar and tire-iron between the two of us—to go clean up her mess. The zombies were disoriented and had lost the trail, but they were still meandering around. Once activated, they'd keep stumbling through the area for a while, and there was always the chance they'd be agitated enough to go for movement if they found any. It was easy enough to sneak up on them and club their heads to slurry for safety's sake, but an unpleasant task indeed. All the more so for its unnecessary nature.

What the hell had she been thinking?

Her rifle and pistol were empty, meaning she'd caught my attention firing the last of her wad. Paranoia and bad-craziness curled through me, as if tiny people were sneaking up on me over my own skin. Who *was* this woman? Shooting zombies was a mug's game. However many there were, more would follow the noise, as they followed any atypical stimuli.

Why would she be here by herself, intent on riling up zombies near where the Minister and I planned to sleep?

Who had sent her, and what did she *know?*

I remember turning from my dark thoughts to see the Minister caught in what I initially took to be his own paranoid spiral, but then I realized his rage had shifted on him again. He was contemplating the unconscious woman and vaguely fingering a small bag he'd carried for years, filled with what the vendor had sworn was genuine Spanish fly.

Then he saw me watching him. An avalanche of expressions crossed his face as he thrust the bag away, out of sight.

"Didn't! Wasn't! Never would!" the Minister cried sharply, before subsiding with a muttered, "Can't be helped."

There was a moment of peace, and then his hand flashed to the fractal-blade he kept on a thong around his neck with a shriek of "Don't you judge me!"

My eyes locked on the intricate blade, glittering in the dying firelight. It was serrated all the way down, and considering the sickly radioactive gleam in the Minister's eyes, more than capable of making me much less pretty. He'd been carrying the damnable knife ever since his sister had used one to cut herself free from a trapped inverted canoe, although he didn't share an interest in that sport or any other.

You must understand that I'd known Minister Dogwood for many years, since high-school in fact, and so I had a firm awareness of just how untrustworthy a fiend I was dealing with.

I pointed the woman's pistol at him, hoping he hadn't seen me check it earlier.

"Back off, you unhinged bastard! I wield *indiscriminate justice!*"

Dogwood's gleaming eyes narrowed, the knifepoint tracing unsteady Moebius strips in the air. Desperate now, I cried, "Go to sleep! What would your mother think?"

A moment of stasis then, before fat tears filled his eyes. He nodded to me once, then climbed sniffling into his sleeping-bag and curled into a ball. I waited for a moment and went for a walk to calm the screaming in my blood, treading on the fallen meaty petals of whatever those poor doomed fantastic things had been.

Something crunched underfoot and I found the shattered remains of the Minister's Lamentable Hat, where it must have been crushed as he wrestled the mysterious woman. I took the loss of the horrible artifact as a good sign for our journey—thankful that the Minister hadn't noticed—and then went to bed myself, suddenly aware of how cold it was and had been for some time.

MORNING WAS A dangerous time for us, full of disorientation and spikes of crystalline suffering into the brain. I felt restrained and lashed out, eventually struggling free of the sleeping bag as from a warmly padded womb. I then made an attempt to remember where I was.

The presence of the woman was very confusing to me.

Who was she?

Had we *done* something?

Her guns and the zombie remnants brought it all back before self-accusation cut too deep, but also raised more questions than were answered. As I considered her, she stirred and woke, clearly with a splitting headache. I sympathized. Our Emergency Glue was not a fun ride, but it did the job.

I poured some water from our rations and set it down where she could get it before drinking some myself. She eyed me warily.

"There were zombies," she said eventually, in an even tone. "Then that maniac attacked me."

"Course they followed you. You sobered up, and were pulling them in from all over."

"*Excuse me?*"

Nonsensical. Perhaps speaking of bad damage. I played along, as patiently as I could.

"They follow you unless you're ripped. Can't shoot them or you attract more. Easy."

I dragged out the breakfast amyls and offered her one. She recoiled.

"What's that?"

"Amyl nitrite. Good for you. Got vitamins."

Nothing in her expression suggested comprehension. I sighed, pondering how a pharmacological virgin could have survived this long. Perhaps she was some Unabomber nutcase only now out of bullets. Since she seemed to be a newbie I took pity and opened one of the bags.

"You're going to have to take something, or the Minister over there is going to wake up and *make* you take something, maybe the glue again, and the glue is a harsh and caustic mistress."

She blinked in silence. I continued.

"We have amyls . . . Mescaline . . . Some weed, but that's recreational rather than safety related . . . The last of the Green Shrieker . . . Some skinpatches with Mayhem Tweed and Strict Blue . . . Some meth, which will sort you out properly but rots your head and your teeth . . . A decent amount of acid and shrooms . . . Hard liquor and speed—"

"—Booze will save you from zombies?"

Incredulous hostility came from her in waves. It gave me a headache, and even more in need of my own dosage.

"Are you *from the past?*" I yelled, grabbing some gear from the supply bags and leaning over the Minister, punching him on the shoulder a few times. "Hang on," I said to her, before returning to Dogwood. "Come on Minister, breakfast dosage!"

He mumbled something unhelpful; I cracked an amyl under his nose and held it there.

"Come on, breathe deep . . . Good man."

He went limp, which is always more comfortable when you're already lying down. I grabbed one myself and turned back to her.

"Anything that'll fuck you up properly will work," I said, aiming for patience. "Booze will do, but you need a lot of it. You'd need to be utterly wasted."

She chewed over the idea, then defaulted to the familiar: "I guess I'll go with the booze."

Handing over a bottle of tequila, I cautioned, "You're going to need to be dedicated

with this, and if they come after you again it's back to the glue."

Gamely enough she took a big swig and grimaced. Hardly surprising; it wasn't very good tequila. I cracked my own amyl and breathed deep, carried away by the biting chemical scent and a delightful tide of dizziness. Purple haze hung in my vision, suspended in a timeless silence in which the world turned around me.

The main wave passed, leaving me with ongoing light-headedness and a sudden awareness of hunger. Food! Yes! I craved sugar and fat, perhaps caffeine. During a visit to the Minister's sprawling family in the U.K. before the dead rose, I had encountered the deep-fried Mars bar: molten delectable battered moneyshots from some chubby god of cardiac arrest. Couple of them, some speed or ecstasy and perhaps a pint or two, and I'd be fuelled for another ten hours of experimental hooliganism.

The Minister maintained the same effect could be achieved with just the speed—with beer to flavor—but the man lacks an artists' soul, any respect for the culinary arts, and a basic knowledge of nutrition.

Alas the issue was moot: there was no access to the pinnacle of Western civilization that was deep-fried chocolate bars. Not without the underlying substrate of Western civilization. That ship had long since sailed, carried away by a rising tide of the walking, hungry dead.

The woman took another swig from the bottle and woke me from my reverie. "If it's just us against the zombies, I'm going to need to know what to call you. I'm Chantal."

"He's the Horse," interjected Dogwood, putting the lie to his apparent coma.

I jerked a thumb at him. "The man who is full of *lies* is Dogwood, my Minister for Lateral Problem-Solving, long term companion and sidekick."

I noticed that the woman had made a healthy dent in the tequila and was looking rather green. Heavy booze on an empty stomach. I saluted her enthusiasm, but she was going to geyser.

"Whoa!" said I, "Slow down or you're going to lose it all!"

It was hard to say whether she heard me. Wordlessly Dogwood began loading our gear into the car and started the long road to actually getting the engine running.

"Why are you two out here?" she asked, clearly bilious. "Where are you going?"

"The Minister and I are on a quest for more Safety Drugs for our community of Bad Axe."

"We're heroes," Dogwood said sagely, fiddling vaguely with the car.

"We head west, seeking population centers which might have a pharmacological bounty for us. But not into central Chicago itself. No, that might be a little *too* exciting. We seek the outlying regions."

Dogwood added, "Detroit would have been *way* too exciting."

I saw in that moment that she understood, but in retrospect it was probably somewhere between my experience with the amyl, and hers with rising bile. She took another swig and shuddered.

"So that's your plan? Survivors just taking drugs forever?"

The Minister and I exchanged a glance and started to laugh. It was not an unreasonable question. Hell, I'm the first to admit that we had not hit upon an ideal long-term solution. Kids, for example. Kids could not be expected to be as Resilient as the Minister or myself, and yet the situation remained. Any given babies had the choice of being pulled apart like some struggling, gut-filled jelly-donuts, or growing into dribbling addicts with skulls full of bad cheese.

I'm not saying we had the answers then, but this was a bridge to cross another day. However, Chantal had inadvertently stumbled onto the larger path that the Minister and I walked, a noble plan to which our current holy mission was but one small part.

"Nah," Dogwood said, "We're going to get Twisted."

It was a simple statement, perhaps *too* simple by the blankness in Chantal's eyes, and as Dogwood said it he popped the engine cover. At the time I wasn't paying attention, but in hindsight the signs of the car's doom were all there. But leaving that aside, the Minister was absolutely right. Our larger quest was to get Twisted, like those noble leaders of men, Presidents Ozzy and Tommy Lee. I believe myself to have been more attached to the notion and disciplined in its pursuit than Minister Dogwood, even then.

"Twisted," I said sagely, "Is when you take enough different drugs over enough time that you—you—"

"Smell different than people," called Dogwood, from somewhere inside the car.

"—*Thank you*, Minister—enough that your body-chemistry changes. Then they never find you, even if you're straight."

Dogwood straightened up and mused, "Sounds useful, but I don't see the point of that bit."

As I say, the Minister lacks true vision.

I remember waxing lyrical, but can't remember precise details. To be Twisted is to be truly free in this new benighted world of ours, untouched by the dead. Transcending natural human body-chemistry to become divine acid-casualties walking the world at will, spreading the word. Why do you think Ozzy and Tommy Lee are probably President? Nobody wants a Commander-in-Chief who might get eaten. It's just sense.

I was about to go into my theories about why cocaine doesn't seem to work when the Minister proclaimed, "Car's buggered."

He was right. Upon investigation, the battery reeked of sulfur.

I'm sure that to someone who knows anything about cars, that'd mean something important. As it was, we were instantly reduced to moving by foot.

"Everything out of the car, Minister," I said, knowing he was already working on it. "This will not slow us down, for we are Resilient."

"True," he said, "Unless you mean in overland speed."

Manfully, I ignored him, for we did actually have a plan. I went for our supply bags. Moving by foot was going to expose us to more zombies, so we needed something good and nasty, with fundamental endurance of effect. I went for the acid; the Minister went for a skinpatch of the Mayhem Tweed. He slapped the patch onto a forearm, giving himself a temporary tattoo like a piece of living couch or librarian's jacket which sank slowly beneath his skin. Dogwood's face flushed and paled in rapid succession while his irises bloomed darkness.

"That's good Tweed," he breathed. I eyed him sidelong while peeling a decent chunk of blotter free. Under Tweed, he was going to need watching, but that was hardly new. After the amount of acid I was intent on taking, I wasn't going to be up for sainthood myself.

Chantal hid behind her tequila bottle when I offered her the bag, drinking more before vomiting copiously into the bushes. With the wad of blotter tucked into one cheek, I began sizing up westward angles to take—it's always easier to take downhill trends on acid—when she spoke up and wiped her lips.

"You're looking for drugs, right?"

The Minister and I exchanged a glance. "Why?"

"Jackson. Lots of drugs in Jackson." She straightened up and took another pull from the bottle. "Police station lockup is full of stuff. I just came from there."

Dogwood snorted. "Bollocks you did, not on foot. That's way the hell back east and—"

"—You have a better idea?"

He deflated with a shrug and looked at me.

"She raises a compelling point."

So without a better idea of destination, and a limited timeframe to decide before polysyllabic demons got a vote, Jackson it was.

* * *

RETRACING THE PATH towards Jackson wasn't hard. The trail of patient zombie steps and sporadic corpses was pretty clear, but six hours of blisters later and the Minister was on the verge of mutiny. A rising column of anger seethed from him and stained the sky above the bleeding footsteps left in his wake.

The Tweed had taken him to a dark place without words or otherwise numbed his tongue. He stalked in silence over the dusty ground while the world throbbed and hummed nameless tunes around us. Chantal obliviously clutched her bottle like a savage cactus-based teddy-bear. She was a metronome vomit-fountain, staining the dust with stinking neon horrors that ate into the ground and sang of vague malevolence.

Me? I just felt kind of mellow.

The air was filled with the scent of dust and dry vegetation, along with crushed parsley and burning insulation rising in waves from the Minister's every bleeding footstep.

It was when the ground stood up and started yelling that I thought I was really freaking out. I can't explain the terror I felt when vaguely humanoid figures the color of dirt were suddenly *there*, shedding dust and trailing vines, reeking of anger and the cruelty man poured into the very soil.

Several things happened in rapid succession.

The Minister collapsed into a paralyzed crouch, a high keening in his throat, his eyes glistening white with fear as the compost beasts came for us.

I screamed in what I was later assured was an appropriately masculine manner.

Chantal dropped her bottle, raised her hands and said, "They're harmless, sir! Phillips reporting!"

One of the creatures spoke, each word a hideous Darth Vader rasp of Inescapable Doom. It was at that point I believe I dropped to the dirt and began to grovel, but in a clearer mind I remember it said, "Christ, Phillips. You go for bullets and find mouths."

"Civilian drug-fiends, sir. They saved me . . ."

The conversation was ongoing, but I stopped paying attention when I noticed the monsters encircling the Minister as he wailed wordlessly against their dusty existence. The outrage pulled me to my feet.

"You can't have him!" I roared. "He's *mine!*"

Chantal and the dirt-beast looked around.

"Mother of—" it said, pausing before making a cutting motion. "Fine. We'll sort these two out. You smell of puke."

"They think intoxication keeps them safe, and weren't happy unless I played along . . . I drank enough that I kept throwing up most of it."

Treachery!

The thought thrilled electrically through me, but by now I was already making efforts to dodge the monsters coming after me like they were herding a rabbit. The *wrongness* of their presence made me shrill and dizzy, but I am no rabbit.

Some fiend threw a sack over my head, the fabric membranous and alive, softly mewling. I crashed to the ground and hauled part of it off in time to see one monster touch the Minister.

The physical contact told him whatever he was seeing was tangible. In an instant he went from paralyzed silence to a gargling howl. One hand flashed to the fractal-blade at his throat and then he waded into the offending monster's leg like a kid into red-spurting birthday cake.

Shouts, then. Noise and bad confusion.

NEXT THING I remember is finding myself in restraints on a gurney.

A relief. This had happened before.

But where was the Minister?

I shifted as the restraints would allow, and there was no sign of Dogwood. Some medical personnel were dickering nearby, a woman and middle-aged man. I overheard, "—what Phillips says it's a miracle they survived this long, but we'll soon sort them out."

"You can't threaten me!" I shouted, channeling the stern hybrid spirit of Clint Eastwood and Charlton Heston. "I deal with scarier things than you in my shoes every morning, and that's only the stuff that's *real!*"

He knelt down beside the stretcher then, one of those paternal doctors you just want to dose with something vivid and enduring, then set free in a shopping mall. We'd see who's so smug *then*.

"My poor boy," he said truculently, "What have you been doing to yourself?"

"No negotiation with terrorists, doc! Return my Minister to me immediately, and we'll be on our way."

"In your current state, you'll poison any Reanimates who bite you!" he laughed, rotund and jocular.

"Ha. Ha. Yes. I fucked your daughter."

I could see this statement displeased him as he backed away, so I tried to figure out these restraints now that I lacked his gaze. Curses! The Minister was much more talented than I in this area. I fiddled and tested and pulled, only to overhear:

"—flush their systems and clean out the muck, straighten them out good and proper."

"Wait, what?"

Silence and blankly hostile faces. The Fear began to rise in me from some chill and murky underground well.

They couldn't do that! They mustn't! I was so close to being Twisted I could taste it in the very air. A few more months! That was it! The Minister and I had started on this path long before the zombies provided a reason.

We were *ahead of the game!*

It became obvious that I was thrashing and probably yelling when they came with glinting unfriendly needles to silence my uncomprehending horror.

I howled out, "The drugs are good for

meeeeeee!" before icy oblivion climbed up a vein, put the chairs on the tables and turned out the lights.

I WOKE TO the smell of smoke, who knows how long later, under a sense of vague, watery sedation. Unrestrained, which meant they were getting careless or trusting, but confronted with a mutinously solid door. However, I guessed that the smoke meant that the Minister was nearby, and about to teach them Proper Caution.

I dragged myself upright and everything felt wrong. The criminals had leached the drugs from my system and replaced them with weakness—fat and heavy metals, weighing me down. Peering through the door's little window, I banged and hollered as best I could: "Fire! You can't leave me in here with this maniac! *Fire!*"

A disorganized pack of people came and let me out, suspicious but fundamentally uninformed of my basic nature. There was something on the air along with the smoke, some primal trapped terror and confusion. These people had far bigger problems at the moment than even myself and the Minister could provide. It was at that moment I remember thinking that we might get out of this yet.

We'd had a lot of practice dealing with panic and disorder as it all came down, and this felt like a flashback or a sequel. First thing's first, however, I had to locate Dogwood. I harnessed my rescue crew with a cry of "Dear Lord! Smoke!" and ran towards it, leaving nothing more than a startled, "Hey, wait!" in my wake. I figured they'd be keeping the Minister nearby, and that if I could keep these people off-balance enough, they'd forget to be too suspicious.

The smoke coincided with frantic hammering on a heavy door. I turned to the confused pack following me and cried, "What are you waiting for? Get the poor man out!"

Dogwood tumbled to the concrete and linoleum-tile of the corridor through thick smoke as the door opened, half-naked and

wheezing, grabbing my leg.

"They tried to kill me, Horse!" he coughed. "Locked me in and left me to burn!"

"No more of that 'Horse' garbage, understand?" I hissed in his ear before straightening to proclaim, "This man is ill and my responsibility—"

But my words were interrupted as the Minister coughed till he was sick on my foot.

"Look," a haggard youth said, unshaven and reeking of The Fear. "We don't care about whatever line of bullshit you're trying to spin. It doesn't matter. And just trust me when I say you'll fight with all the rest of us when the time comes."

I nodded busily, grinning in what I hoped was a manner that spoke of agreement and total comprehension: "Indeed! Fighters, us. Stern repose. All that stuff."

It seemed that we'd been less clever than I'd thought, but they really believed something terrible was coming. It seemed best to trust them on this, and just focus on getting the hell out of Dodge before it arrived. The Minister caught my attention again with another coughing fit, making me pull my foot out of range. His eyes rolled pink like an agitated lab-mouse, wearing nothing but boots and jeans, both legs torn raggedly so that one ended above the knee and the other courted indecency.

"Where are your clothes, Minister?"

"Burned 'em. Had to start somewhere."

Of course he had, but it couldn't be helped. Definitely time to be moving on, away from this foreign place and its aura of doom.

Wait, where *are* we, I thought?

The Minister and I staggered from the concreted area of our incarceration—gray, glass and steel—only to find ourselves on the third storey of an incomprehensible madhouse, when we could see the ground. Vast walls and fences surrounded an area of something akin to four blocks, teeming with shanty structures and fetid masses of humanity. Buildings, clearly pre-existing the Reanimates or whatever these guys

called zombies, hauled themselves up out of the complicated mass below. Few people were left at ground level, seeming to prefer to get as high as they possibly could.

What kind of lunacy *was* this?

Why were they all trying to get off the ground? It looked safe. Or were they looking out over the walls, and if that was the case, why were they freaking out so much?

The furled edges of a conclusion touched my mind, but I will admit that Dogwood got there before I did and saved us the trip upstairs to investigate.

"They've got zombies. A scorching case."

Of course. All of Chantal's weird behavior and the incomprehensible drug-theft treachery could fit if these misguided cretins *were* from the past, and simply hadn't noticed that pattern. Morons.

This was something out of *Mad Max*. Razor-wire and gun-emplacements at the top of the wall, never mind that the repetitive noise would bring them in like nothing else. Well, excepting the smell of legion overheated unwashed humans, or maybe concentrated brain-radiation, or whatever it was they homed in on.

In any case, this place was sun-ripened spam in a can.

It was time to run away.

"You're right, Minister! My god, these people are going to get us both killed!"

"Bad scene, man," he grated on a smoke roughened throat. "Irresponsible."

"Indeed! We need to get to the ground and get out before the zombies arrive."

"What if they're at the gates already?" he clutched my arm. "We might *smell of food!*"

A chill went through me, reminding me of how physically dissolute and watery I felt, sapped of Power and Resilience. A conundrum.

"These people will stockpile gear, Minister. For one thing, they'll have ours. That should be enough to get free of this place. We must find it!"

The two of us slinked and reeled down

sets of stairs to reach the ground, passing or jumping barriers across the stairs when we found them. We were straight-sober for the first time in living memory and the experience was ghastly, stripping away all the filters sane humans need to function and setting us loose like panicky rats under snake-eyes. There was nothing on these levels but shoddy hotel-sized units turned apartment shanty-towns. Not what we needed. I remember peering over banisters and scanning around for a structure that would predate the Big Zs. It'd be run down and blocky. Utilitarian. Just *scream* 'police.'

In the end, the Minister found it by falling down the stairs. He came to rest and, when the swearing died down, reported that there were low windows at the street, containing a six inch view of what looked like cells. And the Minister knew cells.

Breaking into police stations turned out to be surprisingly easy when all the police are AWOL for fear of flesh-rending horrors. I was bent on getting the lock picked or finding something to chisel the hinges when the Minister kicked in one of the ground windows and climbed inside.

"Minister!" I said, scrambling down to the window, "We want to avoid jail cells, and you don't like them. Been very clear on that in the past . . ."

"Door's open, Horse . . ." came the muffled response.

I dislike crawling over even the most tidily broken glass, but truly these were Desperate Times. Dogwood was missing, as happened frequently in times of stress and confusion, but would not stray far. I could hear him scuffling around somewhere beyond the cells, which were indeed open.

I called, "Find anything?"

"Cops stop filing when the world starts to end. Guess it's been ending here for a while."

The man can be a poet when he wants, when the demons aren't soiling that part of his mind, or riding him around the city like a radioactive jet-propelled scooter bent on

mass destruction.

The *real* question was, where would they have put our stuff? Or failing that, where would they have been keeping *other people's stuff*, which we could then get into and abscond with? The search took some time, from memory, leading two increasingly desperate men—both of whom were in the early depths of different flavored DTs as the sedation wore off—through a plethora of pathologically dull police rooms. By a process of elimination we found an evidence lock-up, and it was there that the dark gods smiled upon us with their blackened grimy teeth and decided we'd suffered enough. If the cops had still been in a filing mood we might never have found it, but getting into all the lockers and drawers meant that we located bags that looked *suspiciously* like our supplies. The Minister was even re-united with his fractal-blade, still rusty with monster juice or—in retrospect—soldier blood. He returned it to its thong, and to the gap it left in the tan around his neck. All of the Safety Drugs were there, tagged and dated in little plastic bags.

And then we noticed all the other stuff in the locker. In little plastic bags. And in the lockers next to ours.

They say when it rains it pours, and *howling crackbaby CHRIST* but it was beautiful. My mouth went dry as the Minister began to laugh a low, dirty chuckle.

It was more than we could carry by a significant margin, such riches that to take all of it would have been lamentable greed. The Minister and I were and are pillars of the global community and would not dream of it.

"We *have* to try some of this . . ." the Minister said.

"Indeed! It's medicinal! Choose your weapons and see what you can find by way of a wheel-barrow or box mover, something wheeled." I grabbed a decent chunk of acid and some speed. "Take what you want, Minister; we're making up for lost time and need to be safely wasted by the time the

zombies get in."

He rooted in the bins and suddenly looked up. "They'll be agitated when they arrive. Won't matter if we're wasted so long as we're moving!"

A relevant, alarming point. "True. Drugs, a barrow and a stolen car, Minister. We have our mission."

We didn't find anything so useful as a wheeled box conveyance, but I did find some decent back-packs and a roll of carpet from the adjoining office, which I figured might be useful for getting over any barbed wire. However, in the time it took me to return, the Minister had chosen to plunge us forward once again into Interesting Times.

Different shades of upholstery fabric crawled detectably up each arm and stained his torso, with a third mounting one leg. His eyes were intense and manic, shining with an unwholesome inner light.

I shudder thinking about it, even now. Little will make a grown man more foolhardy, unstable and depraved than mixed, conflicting Tweed. And from the way the cloth pattern stain was spreading, all were unusually high doses.

The plan had changed, although the overall mission remained the same: complete all objectives before Minister Dogwood became a portal for horror and bad confusion to enter this benighted world.

How long could I keep control of my own demons, I wondered? The gust-front of the acid was curling through my brain like a serpent returning to a comfortable lair, and pretty soon it was going to take the wheel.

Here I was, responsible for Minister Dogwood, currently the human equivalent of a dirty suitcase-nuke with a low timer and nothing but red wires. The two of us trying to get out of an armed compound before an unspecified number of the undead—an unknown distance away—broke inside, and all before the acid-snake took me for a joyride.

It is challenges which make us grow.

A SUSURRUS OF voices and the sharp taps

of gunfire carried in the air when we managed to get out of the police station. The cell windows were much too high to escape from the inside, so we had to use the door. Far above, I could see the arms and gestures of the milling throngs as they surveyed their impending doom arriving on implacable rotting legs. No idea how long we had, so safest to assume not much time at all and then work from there.

"Minister," I declared, trying to keep him focused, "Look for vehicles."

I was aware myself of the incipient dust melting into an iridescent sheen and climbing slowly up our legs.

Dogwood's gaze was fixed on the balconies above, apparently on a once-fat woman with sagging bundles of flesh holding onto a malnourished Pomeranian.

"Dogsa darkmeat, yeh?"

Sinking feeling, or was that the melting dirt? Our downward spiral begun so soon? Had to keep him focused, and that would be increasingly difficult.

"No good, Dogwood. Too many bones."

"Can't trust the bones, no."

"Cars, Minister! Focus."

We were attracting attention and shouts from the people above, but that wasn't the real concern. I had to think. Cars would be outside the camp to give them space and since zombies wouldn't damage them, so we had to seek a way out of these hideous walls. The Minister was following me and I wasn't worried about anyone here interfering with him. Mostly naked except for lopsided torn pants, clashing upholstery patterns crawling under his skin and mixing in his torso, brightly maniacal eyes and a fixed grin . . . He was obviously far too crazy a person to mess with. The Tweed patterns were a biological warning to predators, part of how the world declares Do Not Disturb. He was like some feral fusion-powered couch-based Frankenstein lurching around this little settlement in defiance of God's laws, and daring polite society to form a mob. Fortunately, polite society had bigger concerns.

Our wanderings lead us to a change from concrete to hurricane fencing, beyond which the horizon could be seen behind indistinct humanoid figures in the distance. Progress at last! I climbed up enough to throw our carpet over the sharp wire, then hurled the gear bags I was carrying over the fence to the other side. I hoped the Minister would follow my lead, but I was beset by traitorous whispers. Setting him loose here would be like throwing a sack of weasels into a kindergarten; it would definitely afford time for my own escape, but I couldn't do that! He was my Minister, and the crazy bastard for all his faults didn't deserve that. And these poor misguided swine didn't deserve *him*, not in this state.

I climbed the fence, the wire under my hands throbbing with a giant, slow heartbeat and singing in a phantom wind. I was aware of hostile attention from the crowds above and hurried, aiming to cajole Dogwood across once I was on the other side. As I reached the dirt I saw him throw his arms wide and look up at the crowds before booming, "Don't worry, citizens! We're not the undead!"

Thank you, Minister. I remember thinking. *Succinctly put.*

"Come on, throw me the gear and climb over," I yelled. I could see Chantal moving our way through a growing crowd daring the balconies of the lower levels, but ignored her. Dogwood, however, was confused by my interruption.

"What? Why are we leaving? Have you *caved in* to these people?"

"Over the fence, you animal! We don't have time for games!"

Dogwood glared intensely and began to climb, still carrying all his bags. He fought his way up to the carpet, his underskin patterns growing out behind him as membranous fabric wings while my pulse roared and sang in my ears.

Hold it together, I thought. *Maintain!* I thought.

Lose control now and the two of you will

be lost in the storm.

When the Minister came down, the carpet came with him. Shrieking, he rolled in its embrace, punching and biting. I hauled it away and Dogwood looked up at me with huge, mad eyes.

I dragged him bodily away from the fence and looked for vehicles. As I did, the community's situation became clearer. They were in a box-canyon, so the gunshot echoes would summon zombies for miles. The initial forerunners of the undead horde dropped like ripe rupturing fruit as they reached the range of the guns, but that was a finite solution at best—particularly given their thickening crowds. Despite the pace they were being cut down, the mob was still making visible if very slow progress towards the walls. And then they'd start to climb each other.

The two of us had seen this before.

Well, not with the whole *Mad Max* walls and gun-emplacement thing, but otherwise we'd seen it.

The car-pool was dusty and some of the vehicles looked dilapidated, but that'd never stopped us before. I unleashed the Minister and directed him to the nearest jeep. He was always better with hotwiring than me, even while chemically unbalanced.

I watched the man plunge beneath the dashboard and rip into the wires there with a high, tearing scream of laughter. Perhaps, I thought, this time he was too far gone. Yet this was negative thinking and of no purpose. The jeep had some big water tanks strapped to the side which sounded full, and a pile of silver-wrapped food packs in the back. Food and water would be useful if we wanted not to have to drink our piss before we reached civilization.

Never fun.

The engine turned over with a zapping scream, matched with a cry from Dogwood, who began punching the dashboard and swearing. He seemed to have the situation in hand, and my attention was drawn back to the walls of the bleak settlement that was

doing everything wrong.

Poor, misguided, uncomprehending wretches. Trapped in a new world they didn't understand, and much of which wanted to consume their living flesh. A very bad scene today, fear in the air, yet another apocalypse the Minister and I had to witness. The acid hummed, spat and whispered that perhaps this was no accident. Were we the karmically-invested sin-eaters of an entire way of life?

Troubling thought, but I doubted it. We didn't really know these people, not even Chantal.

Chantal.

My eyes narrowed as a conclusion formed, even if I wasn't completely conscious of it at the time. Chantal was a crystalline example of this community. Misguided, unheeding, desperately human, and seeking a means to continue that state. She had a face, particularly in comparison to everyone else the Minister and I had dealt with here, all of whom realistically had been total dicks.

She had a face and a name even if we didn't know her, and she deserved another chance. By extension, so did the rest of them.

I clambered around to the back of the jeep and rooted around for tools, spooking the Minister. He brandished a pair of pliers at me from the floor and weaved dangerous, eerie patterns in the air with the shining points, like a crab signaling territory over lake mud.

These people *were* organized. There were two sorts of tire-iron, and right where they should be, rather than under the seats or taped to the bodywork. I grabbed the longer one that was unimpeded by a crosspiece, and set out at an angle that would bring me towards the thickening tide of zombies while keeping me visible to the watchers above.

The chattering of the idiot guns was still keeping them far enough back that it was a long walk in the afternoon sun, any moment expecting a stray round. The acid wave hit and broke over me en route, melting the ground into a thick stodgy soup and staining the sky with strobing neon torment. An endless staticky hiss filled the world, like a bad recording of surf on a stony eternal shore. The zombies seemed to join the soup, reminding me of the ghastly visions which beset me when Chantal lead us into that trap.

For a moment I contemplated going back and ceasing my rebellion against The Fear, soured by memory of that betrayal. But no! I would be holy Teflon to that ugliness, and refuse to soften my resolve.

The lecherous, biting gunfire laughter stopped altogether as I neared and singled out one particular zombie, which at least suggested they'd noticed me and cared. I was touched. Then they started up again, to chew away at the fringes some distance from me.

I focused on my target as the viscous world lurched, bubbled and sang.

You can't trust the dead. For every staggering Romero-brand which saps your caution, you'll find another one fresh enough to run screaming or throw something. Or one dried by desert winds into staggering carnivorous cordwood, seemingly harmless till they get close enough to release the crossbow tension in twisted tendons like steel cables and rip you in half. And then occasionally you find a zombie with activated Augments and implants. If you're wary you have a very bad day. If you're not wary you probably don't get a *chance* to have a bad day.

Even if you're ripped or Twisted, there are few guarantees. Not when you're up close and personal, and particularly not when they can smell flesh on the wind.

The one I'd singled out was dry and old, but lively enough. His stiffened leathery skin—all in patches—creased into a frown as he neared me, aware I was there but not what I was. I steeled myself and held out an arm before the creature, watching its rotting nostrils flex in and out, wuffling around and searching for this weird thing I was. Those horrible nostrils! They unfurled slowly like miniature elephant trunks on the hunt, or seemed to, sparking thrills of nauseous horror. I didn't move except to turn back to the walls and balconies where binoculars winked.

Backing a safe distance away from the hideous, duel-elephant thing, I pointed and roared, "See? No bitey!"

At the noise, all the zombies recalibrated to me, until the settlement fired again and refocused them on the walls. With luck, the villagers finally noticed that part of the pattern. I moved back to the zombie I'd initially targeted and smacked it in the skull with the tire-iron till it stopped moving. The body smelled like opening a bag of jerky which has started to turn—dry, salty and corrupt. It took me back to that god-awful bar in Terra Haute, with gleaming soiled gems of teeth and enamel fragments in the urinal, but I forced the memory down and decided to drive the point home to these people. After all, they were woefully behind the times.

I spent five or ten minutes running through this forest of corpses and played the Minister's games. I pushed them over like tipping humanoid cows, danced around before them, safe in their confusion, and even tied one's shoelaces together to leave it stumbling and crawling. Nothing without risk, but I was high on superiority.

Puffed by my Heroic Exertions, I moved back toward the settlement to see results. People with rifles were watching me, one with binoculars. Chantal was also in evidence with that group. As I watched, one of the armed figures turned to the man with the binoculars and spoke.

Instantly, I knew what was said, like a voice from over my shoulder stating in a reasonable tone, "Maybe we should shoot him?"

Paranoia gripped me in a cold, thorny fist. A finger lanced out at Chantal.

"Her!" I screamed. It took a second or two for the sound to hit the balconies. "Indeed! She's seen it! Ask her!"

Already she was engaged in conversation with Official Looking People, perhaps to deny knowing me. It was hard to say. But it can be very hard to stop talking when acid is at the wheel, words tumbling out despite my terror that I was only making things worse.

"The police station! Full of glorious drugs to keep you safe! More than you need! And *stop shooting at them!*"

People on the move, either towards their miraculous drug cache or to come get us.

It was Time to Leave.

I ran back towards the jeep, finding the engine running and the Minister strapped securely into the passenger seat, grinning alarmingly and showing bright teeth. His eyes held mine, inhuman intensity and mirth unblinking in shining white orbs. I'd seen that stare. Hell, I've *stared* that stare, and it is a noted harbinger of nothing good. No matter, I thought. A problem for another time, and we had many miles to travel yet.

Climbing into the driver's seat, I made sure that the supplies were actually *in* the car. Dumping the soiled tire-iron in the back, I floored it, sending us towards more comprehensible climes in a cloud of dust—or would do, as soon as I figured out where we were. Chantal had mentioned Jackson, but was this another Unfortunate Lie?

I considered the situation as we drove into the golden heat of the late afternoon sun. The growl of the engine thrummed through the very ground until the sky itself coruscated to its tone before the two of us, a pair of Chemical Saints, mission accomplished and returning home—as soon as we found it.

Warily, I also kept an eye on the Minister as he savaged open the packaging on a Meal Ready-to-Eat with his fractal blade.

It was serrated, you see.

All the way down. ☮

Kevin Veale has had fiction published in *Androm-*

TELL=TALE HOMES

Meet Edgar Allan Poe, world=class vagrant.

FOR WRITERS, EDGAR Allan Poe is a hard man to avoid, especially if that writer happens to live on the East Coast of the United States. Not just because Poe created the genre of mystery fiction, founded modern horror by eliminating the moral instruction formerly universal in such stories, and also planted the seed of science fiction. Poe is hard to avoid because Poe was a failure.

There's a plaque in Boston, a cottage in the Bronx, a building in Philadelphia that has gained the status of National Historic Site, the grave in Baltimore, and a museum in Richmond, Virginia. But Poe isn't a George Washington figure; important though he is to American culture, we don't need ten thousand signs detailing places where Poe might have slept. There are a ton of Poe residences and other remembrances partially because Poe moved around a lot in his adult years. Edgar Allan Poe attempted the impossible—to make a living as a writer and editor in the United States during an era

when English-language publishing was dominated by the United Kingdom.

When I first visited the Poe cottage in the Bronx, I was impressed. It was a tiny home—small rooms and a half-attic that served as bedrooms for Poe and his wife/cousin Virginia, and Virginia's mother. The ceiling nearly scraped against the top of my head—and I am not a tall man—and I could have laid down across the parlor and with my arms outstretched hit two walls; but it was still a house. At the time, I was paying $900 a month for a extremely dubious "two-bedroom" apartment in Jersey. Poe's cottage would have gone for $4,000 easy, in the Bronx. Stick it in Manhattan, that cottage would have been a five-digit rent, if it were first outfitted with electricity and heat. And that's not counting the basement, in which the park ranger that manages the cottage sleeps as part of the salary for the gig.

But the cottage, which cost Poe $400 a year, was a nineteenth-century dump. Poe biographer Kenneth Silverman quotes a visitor who said, "You wouldn't have thought decent people could have lived in it." Indeed, the home's long-term survival is explained by the fact that the cottage was miserable and located in an out-of-the-way suburb. It was easy to move to a nearby park when some apartment buildings went up, though *Life* magazine had to sponsor a campaign to save the structure. A young Jim Thompson was among the thousands who sent in a dollar to save the cottage of his literary hero.

Poe's fortunes were moments of feast interspersed by years of famine. In 1845 alone, Poe lived in three different Manhattan residences: a small house on Greenwich Street, then the three of them together in a boarding house on East Broadway, and finally on nice place in a swanky part of town, 85 Amity Street (now West 3rd). Just a few blocks from Washington Square Park, and owned by New York University, the Poe House, as it was subsequently called, was recently torn down to create a monstrous new building for the law school. After protests by everyone from Lou Reed to the Mystery Writers of America, and the arrest of a demonstrator who recited "The Raven" through a megaphone, NYU decided to keep the façade of the building and integrate it into the new structure. The end result is the sort of disaster one might end up with after the power goes out and one has to eat whatever is in the fridge for dinner—corn and bacon for everyone! Demolished in 2001, this house was the last extant Poe building in Manhattan.

Other cities have had a bit more luck preserving their Poe. The site at 530–532 North 7th Street, Philadelphia, was declared a national memorial by

Poe's travels up and down the crooked little vein of America were fueled by the most practical of issues: he couldn't pay the damn rent.

Congress in 1980. Poe lived in Philly for nearly six years and spent eighteen months in this building, a near-record given the number of times he was forced to move by angry landlords and failed publishing schemes. The relative stability of his homestead and Philadelphia's reputation as the publishing center of the United States did help—Poe wrote over thirty short stories while in Philly, including "The Murders in the Rue Morgue," and three books. Too bad for Poe the books were the no-advance, no-royalty deals not unusual back when the distinction between a printer and a publisher was blurry. Philly wasn't full of much brotherly love, either; in the 1840s, the city didn't have a police force, and plumbing was generally a novelty. Crime and filth filled the streets, as did poverty (Poe was hardly alone in his hunger) and racial strife. Poe generally set his stories in pre-contemporary times, or overseas, but much of the Gothic muck of his fiction was in truth just outside his window.

The most famous Poe city is, of course, Baltimore. Poe died there under bizarre circumstances—a disappearance, strange clothes, an Election Day reappearance—and is buried there still. The surviving Baltimore Poe House (oddly, also on an Amity Street) was actually rented by his aunt Maria Clemm, who was also the mother of Poe's child bride Virginia, in 1832. Poe was in his early twenties and just beginning to make a small name for himself as a writer and editor, the highlight being winning fifty dollars from a local newspaper for "MS Found In A Bottle." By 1836, Poe left for Richmond, Virginia, and the household quickly collapsed—Maria and Virginia followed Poe south. Like other Poe dwellings, the Baltimore house was preserved due to public outcry—most of the surrounding buildings were torn down in the 1930s to make way for a public housing project called the Poe Homes. The area is still fairly seedy, which is a more fitting tribute to Poe than the Baltimore city fathers might wish.

The Richmond Poe Museum is in the Old Stone House, a colonial dwelling that was not a Poe residence. It is located near Poe's Richmond home and the offices of the *Southern Literary Messenger*. What the Museum lacks in authenticity, it makes up for in sheer perversion. Along with the Poeana (a walking stick he forgot to pack!) and first editions is an exhibit of the history of speculations regarding the cause of the poet's death. Beating was an early favorite (1857) and made a comeback late last century (1998).

There are other Poe places. Near the Public Garden in Boston, and just steps away from both Emerson College and the writer's center Grub Street Inc., is a plaque commemorating Poe's birthplace. Manhattan's Edgar Cafe (West 84th Street) was the site of a farmhouse in which Poe wrote most of "The Raven." (Try the key lime pie.) If you ever find yourself in Jersey City, in the bad part of town (Greenville) in a housing development called Currie's Woods, feel free to drink yourself crazy and spend three days and nights running around half-naked and screaming, just like Poe allegedly did in 1842.

There is a dark undercurrent to all of these Poe places. Why so many? Poe was hunting for something in this young America, his own version of the American Dream. He wanted to write, to marry, to be seen as a man of letters and honored for his creativity. Despite his genius, and the flashes of public recognition he received, Poe was never anything more than a genteel bum during his own life, and an incorrigible troublemaker. He picked fights with Longfellow, plagiarized, and used both non-bylined columns and pseudonyms to review his own material. Indeed, Poe once even attacked himself under the name Outis ("Nobody") in order to further his campaign against Longfellow. If he were alive today, Poe might be a minor writer but likely a *major* blogger, punching above his weight class with new controversies and new denunciations every week.

Poe's travels up and down the crooked little vein of America were fueled by the most practical of issues: he couldn't pay the damn rent. He drank heavily, scribbled frantically to keep dimes and dollars flowing in, and lurched from one enterprise to another, none of which cemented his income or his fame. In short, Poe was a loser and a lowlife. A genius, yes, but these other things as well. It's so easy to forget this today, given that Poe is taught rather than read, and nothing transforms the transgressive into the canonical like posthumous acclaim. The truth is in the location of the surviving buildings: Poe lived on the edge, in more ways than one. Every city has its own share of Poe history, but the story is generally the same: swampland and slumlords, and after the bills piled up too high, a midnight ride to somewhere, anywhere, else.

Poe fan Jim Thompson was fond of saying that there was only one plot in all the world: "Things are not what they seem." These dusty Poe places, filled as they are with the echoes of the man and his feather quill, not to mention third-grade class trips, are not what they seem. If Poe were half the man the exhibit copy and museum brochures made him out to be, there would be half as many Poe sites left standing. They are not a tribute to American letters, but instead to the Imp of the Perverse, that little demon that drove Poe to both creative heights and abject depths. Like the Imp himself said, "But why shall I say more? To-day I wear these chains, and am here! To-morrow I shall be fetterless!—but where?" ☉

Nick Mamatas is the author of *You Might Sleep...* and *Move Under Ground*, among others, and the Hugo-nominated former editor of *Clarkesworld Magazine*. His last *Weird Tales* story was "Mainevermontnewhampshiremass" in #350.

Lost in Lovecraft

A GUIDED TOUR OF THE DARK MASTER'S WORLD

BY KENNETH HITE

*"*The year after I first beheld the tomb, I stumbled upon a worm-eaten translation of Plutarch's Lives in the book-filled attic of my home."* —H.P. LOVECRAFT, "THE TOMB"*

Jervas Dudley, the protagonist of Lovecraft's very first piece of adult fiction, "The Tomb," models himself after the Greek hero Theseus and sees "dryads," outbreaks of Classicism spawned and energized by his chance discovery of Plutarch's *Lives of the Noble Greeks and Romans*. As Poe put it, "the glory that was Greece, and the grandeur that was Rome" together make up a stretch of Lovecraft country that we can call (in somewhat, er, antique fashion) Antiquity. It's a space somewhat surprisingly neglected by Lovecraft scholars—and even more surprisingly neglected, at least on the surface, by Lovecraft himself despite his declaration to Clark Ashton Smith: "Classical legend is full of fruitful themes."

"On a verdant slope of Mount Maenalus, in Arcadia, there stands an olive grove about the ruins of a villa. Close by is a tomb, once beautiful with the sublimest sculptures, but now fallen into as great decay as the house. At one end of that tomb, its curious roots displacing the time-stained blocks of Panhellic marble, grows an unnaturally large olive tree of oddly repellent shape…"
—H.P. LOVECRAFT, "THE TREE"

Lovecraft only wrote one tale set in Antiquity, after all, and "The Tree" is far from his strongest work. It's set during the fourth century B.C. on the sacred mountain of Pan, Mount Maenalus, although the narrative drive comes from a liminal space between Greece and Rome: Sicily under the "Tyrant of Syracuse." It's a simple quasi-Gothic shudder-story retold (not particularly compellingly) as a minor Classical fable, but it has an interestingly Love-

craftian trunk within its foliage. Even in this classical Arcadia (literally!) there is corruption and desolation, albeit in this case caused by human motives.

To this solitary fruit, we can add if we like "The Green Meadow," a collaboration with Winifred Virginia Jackson about a Greek savant of the Classical era who is abducted or stumbles into the titular Otherworldly vale. And for the Roman side of things, we might consider "The Very Old Folk," a story fragment about an official of the late Republic who (unwisely, as it turns out) orders a cohort of soldiers to break up a primitive barbarian rite in the Hispanian foothills. "The Very Old Folk" is actually a fixup of a dream Lovecraft had in 1927 and described to many of his correspondents, among them Frank Belknap Long, who eventually turned it into his own story, "The Horror From the Hills."

TO HEAR ANTIQUITY'S CALL

"When about seven or eight I was a genuine pagan, so intoxicated with the beauty of Greece that I acquired a half-sincere belief in the old gods and Nature-sprits. I have in literal truth built altars to Pan, Apollo, Diana, and Athena, and have watched for dryads and satyrs in the woods and fields at dusk."
—H.P. LOVECRAFT, "A CONFESSION OF UNFAITH"

In his letters, Lovecraft makes plain his visceral, emotional connection to Antiquity. He mentions his childhood discovery of Hawthorne's *Wonder-Book* and Bulfinch's *Age of Fable*, his grandfather's tales of Roman travel, and other inspirations including a handful of genuine Roman coins, the memory of which still brought Lovecraft to the verge of ecstasy in a letter written decades later. At the age of seven, he wrote his own version of the *Odyssey* in iambic trimeter. His second childish pseudonym (after "Abdul Alhazred") was "L. Valerius Messala," and while he loved the stories (and eventually the philosophies) of the Greeks, Lovecraft from an early

72 ~ WEIRD TALES ~ Fall 2009

age considered himself a Roman, and repeatedly identified himself as such in his letters. Picking two examples out of many, on November 24, 1927, Lovecraft wrote to Donald Wandrei, "Psychologically, I am either a Roman or an Englishman," and on December 13, 1933, HPL described to Clark Ashton Smith his "natural and unshakeable feeling of being a Roman."

"Anchester had been the camp of the Third Augustan Legion, as many remains attest, and it was said that the temple of Cybele was splendid and thronged with worshippers who performed nameless ceremonies at the bidding of a Phrygian priest. Tales added that the fall of the old religion did not end the orgies at the temple, but that the priests lived on in the new faith without real change. Likewise was it said that the rites did not vanish with the Roman power..."

—*H.P. LOVECRAFT,*
"THE RATS IN THE WALLS"

Thus Lovecraft's fiction generally presents Rome as a synecdoche for "civilization," regardless of the seemingly absurd juxtaposition of alien super-technologists with Iron Age humans. The inhuman nature of the aliens is even refuted by appeal to Rome: in both "The Nameless City" and *At the Mountains of Madness,* archaeologists in denial argue the aliens' horrific self-portraits to be nothing more than artistic conventions like the wolf-symbol of Rome. In the cities of the Great Race of Yith, we are told, "the principle of the arch was known as fully and used as extensively as by the Romans." Like the Romans, the Yithians have howling barbarians penned up — until the barriers fail and civilization is destroyed. In *Mountains of Madness* Lovecraft explicitly compares the stultification of the senescent crinoid Old One civilization in Antarctica (who also "relied on" the Roman arch) to the decadence of Constantine's late-Roman empire, and the crude, imitative bas-reliefs carved by the Old Ones' shoggoth subjects and successors to "ungainly Palmyrene sculptures

Neil Gaiman's NeVer Wear

www.NeVerWear.Net

www.NeVerWear.Net

fashioned in the Roman manner."

The shoggoths in *Mountains* are the cosmic version of the ante-Roman (and anti-Roman) survivals demonized in earlier Lovecraft tales. In "The Horror at Red Hook," the evil cult's lore (and ancestry) comprises a macedoine of Rome's enemies, from Carthage to Persia. In "The Rats in the Walls," the Roman bastion that will become Exham Priory merely covers the horrors below. In The Case of Charles Dexter Ward, Joseph Curwen seeks knowledge of "the Sign of the Goat found on the ancient Roman altar" in a Limoges crypt. The titular scion in the story fragment "The Descendant" comes from decayed Roman stock, which is an aspect of Rome's fall— and of Lovecraft's imaginary landscape— that we'll revisit anon. But for the most part, Lovecraft's horrors are, as he put it in "The Very Old Folk," "dooms which ought not to exist within the territories of the Roman People."

"I believe I did ridiculous things such as offering prayers to Artemis, Latona, Demeter, Persephone, and Plouton. All that I recalled of a classic youth came to my lips as the horrors of the situation roused my deepest superstitions."

—*H.P. LOVECRAFT,*
"THE MOON-BOG"

Five other Lovecraft tales deal with what we might call hauntings from Antiquity: "The Strange High House in the Mist," "The Moon-Bog," "The Temple," "Hypnos," and "Medusa's Coil." Intriguingly, all five are set outside the normal boundaries of the Classical world: Massachusetts, Ireland, the mid-Atlantic, London (a borderline case), and Missouri. (Lovecraft rescues the Atlantis of "The Temple" for Antiquity by assuring the reader that its art was "largely Hellenic in idea . . . the remotest ancestor" of Greece. No pre-human aliens here, unless you count the Dionysian dolphins that follow the U-29.) But all five are clearly Greco-

> *"I have in literal truth built altars to Pan, Apollo, Diana, and Athena, and have watched for dryads and satyrs in the woods."*

Roman in inspiration, form, or both. In the first four, the horror follows the faultless Classical pattern of Nemesis, striking down the hubris of the various unfortunate protagonists. The fifth combines two Greek monsters, the Gorgon and the Lamia, though it doesn't follow the Classical moral or narrative structure.

Even as a specter, Antiquity is not entirely grim: in "Strange High House," Roman Neptune is heralded with "golden flames" and "sportive tritons," while by contrast, Celtic Nodens is "gray and awful." The naiads in "Moon-Bog," both the boy and the idol in "Temple," and the avatar of "Hypnos" are all explicitly described as beautiful. (So, for that matter, is the lamia in "Medusa's Coil.") In other stories, Antiquity merits only a shout-out, a way for Lovecraft to touch his historical bases. Among the kidnap victims in "The Shadow Out of Time" we find a Roman quaestor ("of Sulla's time") and a Greco-Bactrian scribe; in "The Haunter of the Dark," Minoan fishermen rescue the Shining Trapezohedron from the deep. (For what it's worth, on the other end of the time scale, Italians keep the Haunter at bay, although this is almost certainly stretching a point.) The Necronomicon itself, with its Greek-derived name (perhaps a Lovecraftian riff on the first-century Roman poet Manilius' Astronomicon) and its Byzantine provenance, can be seen as the ultimate shout-out to Antiquity despite its medieval origins.

"[E]ven now on Maenalus, Pan sighs and stretches in his sleep, wishful to wake ... In thy yearning hast thou divined what no mortal, saving only a few whom the world rejects, remembereth: that the Gods were never dead, but only sleeping the sleep and dreaming the dreams of Gods in lotos-filled Hesperian gardens beyond the golden sunset. And now draweth nigh the time of their awakening ..."
— *H.P. LOVECRAFT AND ANNA HELEN CROFTS, "POETRY AND THE GODS"*

Or perhaps Lovecraft's ultimate shout-out to Antiquity is the Cthulhu Mythos itself, the body of imaginary lore and legend that HPL explicitly patterned on the chaotic, contradictory matter of Greek mythology. (This is because Greek mythology was the only mythos that Lovecraft knew in any detail, but still.) In his seminal and unconscionably neglected essay "The Cthulhu Mythos," George T. Wetzel pointed out the similarities between, for example, the Dreamlands and the classical Elysium and Tartarus. On the scale of a single story, "The Dunwich Horror" recapitulates and recasts the Greek myths of gods and mortals interbreeding to produce monsters and heroes. Its demigod, Wilbur Whateley, is a twin (like Heracles or Castor), shows prodigious talent as an infant (like Hermes and Heracles), fulfills an oracular prophecy (like Theseus and Jason) and dies torn to pieces (like Dionysos and Orpheus). On a larger scale, Lovecraft's deities resemble the disinterested entities of Epicurus — except for Nyarlathotep, the mocking messenger (Hermes also had a thousand faces), whose vendetta against Randolph Carter might be that of an arbitrary Poseidon against Odysseus. Or look at Lovecraft's collaboration "Poetry and the Gods." The excerpt above lays it out: regardless of what Plutarch heard, the Great God Pan is not dead but sleeping. Dionysos, torn to pieces, will revive. And when he returns, the world will resound with his worshippers' ancient cry: "Ia! Ia!" ℮

YOUR TOUR OF LOVECRAFT COUNTRY BEGINS HERE...

A wide-ranging and friendly journey through H.P. Lovecraft's tales of cosmic terror and wonder, the *Tour de Lovecraft* is the ideal companion to the work of the twentieth century's greatest horrorist.

Kenneth Hite has spent decades reading and re-reading Lovecraft and his heirs, slipping through the forests of verbiage to discover the solid literary ground beneath. With his game designer's eye for structure and connection, in this book he reveals the threads and themes that run throughout Lovecraft's masterpieces. The *Tour de Lovecraft* alternately ambles and careets through all fifty-one of the Master's horror tales in chronological order from "The Tomb" to "The Haunter of the Dark," offering cheerful opinion, incisive literary criticism, playful speculation, and the occasional unhinged rant. It's a response to Lovecraft, and to his occasional humorless critics, that offers you Edmund Burke's Gothic perspective on Cthulhu side-by-side with "The Haunter of the Dark" considered as Grail quest.

"Kenneth Hite's *Tour de Lovecraft* is indispensible. Thorough, insightful, and compellingly readable, it's a perfect introduction for newcomers to Lovecraft and an endlessly fascinating review for long-time Lovecraft addicts. This is *the* companion-book to Lovecraft's fiction—I read it entirely in one sitting, and I know I'm going to read it again many times over the coming years."

—TIM POWERS, AUTHOR OF *DECLARE* AND *LAST CALL*.

AVAILABLE IN BOOK AND HOBBY GAME STORES EVERYWHERE, OR AT WWW.ATOMICOVERMIND.COM

ATOMIC OVERMIND PRESS
143 Wesmond Dr.
Alexandria, VA 22305
USA

Visit us online at
www.atomicovermind.com

WWW.RONINARTS.COM

The Cryptic

BY DARRELL SCHWEITZER

THE ULTIMATE ELDRITCH TOME

TO BEGIN WITH, Centipede Press's *A Lovecraft Retrospective: Artists Inspired by HPL*, released in 2008, is almost certainly the most physically extravagant book in the history of fantasy publishing. It is *massive*. The plainest version of it weighs twelve pounds—even without the slipcase. The trim size is 12 by 15.5 inches. With about 400 pages of glossy paper and a heavy cloth binding, it's two inches thick. Color on almost every page. Brilliant reproduction. Numerous fold-outs. This is more than a bug-crusher, if I may technical language here. ("Bug-crusher" is a useful term coined by Gardner Dozois to describe one of those gargantuan volumes —usually a bloated, unedited novel by a big-name author—which, if toppled over on its side without any additional pressure, will crush a bug.) This is more of an armadillo-crusher, sufficient to crack the chitinous hide of the half-insect, half-fungoid Mi-Go of Yuggoth if you should happen to be careless.

So don't drop it. You can order a copy from Centipede Press, c/o Jerad Walters, at 2565 Teller Ct., Lakewood CO 80214, or you could check out Centipede's Web site at **www.centipedepress.com** and gaze upon page after page of amazingly idealistic publications and proposals, although I suspect you won't be able to order some of the more grandiose ones. While Centipede does offer the occasional paperback, most of its publications are priced in the hundreds of dollars. *A Lovecraft Retrospective*, for instance, sells for $395.00 in the clothbound and slipcased edition, and a whopping $2,485.00 for the ultra-limited, signed, leather, traycased, edition which comes with extra prints. The jaw drops.

Is it worth it? I have not seen the deluxe, twenty-four-hundred dollar edition, but with the "plain" $395.00 edition in front of me as I write this, the answer is, in a word, if you have that kind of money to spend, *yes*. I wouldn't wait for the remainder or for the cheap paperback—this is *the* luxury item for the devoted Lovecraftian. Next to it, a Cthulhu cult statue before which you may perform unspeakable rites is just a trinket. (Centipede offers one of those too.)

You can see from what he publishes that Jerad Walters really enjoys a *fine* book. Every detail matters; he insists on the finest of everything.

To describe the contents of *A Lovecraft Retrospective* a little more closely: There's a preface by Stuart Gordon, who made the *Reanimator* films; an introduction by Harlan Ellison; an afterword by Thomas Ligotti; and artist profiles and commentary by genre experts like Stefan Dziemianowicz and Jane Frank as well as several of the artists themselves. Robert M. Price, one of the great Lovecraft scholars, contributes an essay on the various hoax versions of *The Necronomicon*—with graphics, of course. There is a section on "Early Art," which covers Virgil Finlay, Hannes Bok, Lee Brown Coye, Frank Utpatel, EC Comics, and Richard Taylor. (If this last name doesn't immediately ring a bell, he's otherwise mainstream artist who did some wonderful covers for Arkham House in the '50s and early '60s, for *The Horror from the Hills, The Trail of Cthulhu, The Shuttered Room,* etc.) Tucked in just in front of the Early Art section is a sampling of even earlier illustrations to Lovecraft stories from pulp magazines and 1940s paperbacks, all of it printed to a degree of fineness which would have amazed and dazzled the original artists. Here we get the best reproduction ever of the first genuinely great Lovecraftian painting, the June 1936 *Astounding Stories* cover by Howard V. Brown for "The Shadow Out of Time," depicting the scholar-aliens of the Great Race in their library of 150 million years ago, with a human figure placed among them for scale. On the facing page is Brown's "At the Mountains of Madness" cover, also from *Astounding,* but since the original

Giorgio Comolo's rendition of Cthulhu.

painting may no longer be extant, this is shot from a copy of the magazine itself, and no doubt touched up with Photoshop to get rid of any creases. This is probably the best rendition we will ever see of *that* painting, either, which shows two hapless explorers pursued by a shoggoth that looks like green mucus.

We move beyond this to "Middle" and "Modern" art, with page after page of sumptuous reproductions, both color and black-and-white, of Bernie Wrightson, Helmut Wenske, John Stewart, H.R. Giger (a generous selection from his *Necronomicon*), Stephen Fabian, Michael Whelan, Ian Miller, Allen Koszowski, Les Edwards, Randy Broecker, J.K. Potter, Dave Carson, John Jude Palencar, Bob Eggleton, and many more..

That's a *lot* of Lovecraft art. It's like a massive gallery show, giving the complete history of the development of Lovecraftian illustration and Lovecraft-influenced art. Is all of it great art? As Harlan Ellison points out in his introduction, no. The early Avon cover for *The Lurking Fear* is very close to what Harlan says it is: "apparently rendered by an exceedingly ham-fisted and talentless simian, using only its tail and hind-paws." The Andrew Brosnatch illustrations, from *Weird Tales* in the 1920s, also range from mediocre to awful, his header for "The Music of Erich Zann" being perhaps the single most uninspired piece of fantasy art in the life-cycle of the universe. It is easy to appreciate why fans of the period referred to Brosnatch as "the master assassin" for his ability to completely destroy the point of any story through one of his illustrations. But there are only a couple of these, and they are undeniably of historical importance. Most of the book is simply breathtaking. The range is enormous, from the starkly realistic to the wildly dream-like and surreal, plus one superbly executed joke, Gahan Wilson's famous cartoon from *Playboy* showing Wilbur Whateley as a flasher.

There is much which readers of the more recent *Weird Tales* will recognize, artists who have appeared in the magazine since its revival in 1987: Page after page of finely-rendered Allen Koszowski black & whites including his classic horror feature of "The Shadow Over Innsmouth." Black-and-white and color work from Stephen Fabian (although from *Whispers,* not from *Weird Tales*). A couple Jason Van Hollanders. Jeff Remmer's "Dagon" cover from issue #321. And, outstanding in a book which contains quite a few portraits of the Big Squid Guy, two splendid Cthulhu paintings by Bob Eggleton: one from *Weird Tales* #305, one from the first issue of *H.P. Lovecraft's Magazine of Horror.*

Lovecraft's own illustrative relationship with *Weird Tales* is problematic. His first stories, published during the Edwin Baird editorship, 1923-24, were given absolutely wretched illustrations. But then, so was everything else. It's a sad fact, largely concealed over the years by the rarity and expense of surviving copies, since gradually revealed by facsimile reprints of same—now, from Girasol Collectibles, you can buy reprints at $35 apiece of issues that would otherwise cost you thousands of dollars—that in its first year and a half, *Weird Tales* was an astonishingly ugly, ill-designed magazine, and not very well edited either. The literary quality soared when Farnsworth Wright took over in late 1924, but the artwork did not improve nearly as rapidly. While some of Hugh Rankin's charcoal drawings must have seemed effectively atmospheric at the time, the ones we see here, such as that for "The Dunwich Horror," still come off as marginally promising amateur work, particularly in the context of a book like *A Lovecraft Retrospective.* The magazine did not consistently feature competent art until the mid-1930s, and, apart from a couple J. Allen St. John covers, nothing that could be described as really outstanding until the advent of Virgil Finlay in 1936. Up to that time, by far the best Lovecraft art published anywhere was the two covers for HPL's two appearances in *Astounding.*

Curiously, for all he was very popular among *Weird Tales* readers at the time, Lovecraft was never given a cover in his lifetime. This may well be because the 1930s' idea of what sold pulp magazines had to do with scantily-clad ladies in jeopardy or bondage, and Lovecraft stories notably lacked these elements—quite unlike those of, say, Robert E. Howard, who was not above deliberately writing a lesbian whipping scene into a Conan story in order to capture the cover. The prim and puritanical Gent from Providence would never so lower himself. But as a result, the original, pulp *Weird Tales* is not all that fully represented in *A Lovecraft Retrospective.* There is only one cover, not a very good one, showing two Deep Ones from "The Shadow Over Innsmouth"; this was used only on the Canadian edition of *WT* in 1942. The only other cover HPL ever got was by Virgil Finlay, illustrating the poem "Hallowe'en in a Suburb," on the September 1952 issue. It's not here, possibly because the original does not survive and reproduced magazine covers seem below par in this book, or possibly because the compilers didn't think it among Finlay's best. (I don't either.) While a great deal of the significant Lovecraftian illustration of the past eight-four years is gathered here, no one could reasonably expect it *all* to be.

One of the things we conclude from this book is that the real blossoming of Lovecraftian graphic art came a generation and more after his death. There were few good illustrations in the pulp magazines, mostly by Finlay and Bok, then stirrings in the '50s and '60s, but nothing exploded until at least the '70s. This coincides with the permeation of Lovecraft's influence throughout the culture generally; as he became a major, worldwide figure, more and more competent and even brilliant artists were drawn to and inspired by his work. The result is a lot more

It's like a massive gallery show, giving the complete history of the development of Lovecraftian art.

 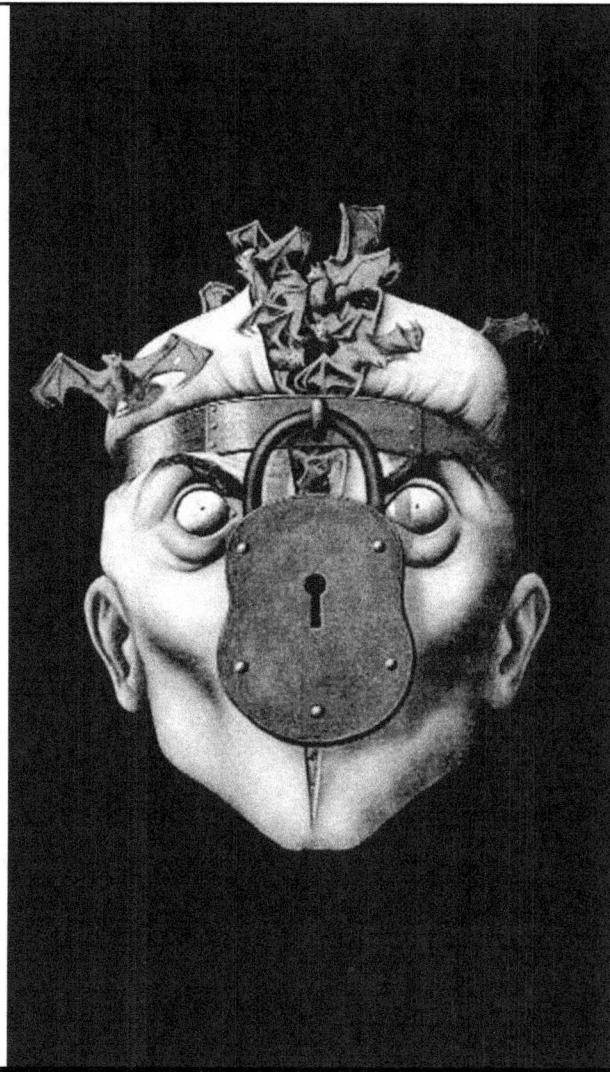

Pooch's "Tunnel of Lovecraft" (left) and the classic cover of Lovecraft's *The Tomb* (right).

than just a collection of paintings of rampaging calamari. It is an expression of the unique and powerful Lovecraftian vision, filtered through numerous other sensibilities. If you were to go back in time and tell Lovecraft that a genius Swiss surrealist painter named H.R. Giger, not yet born when Lovecraft was alive, would one day paint a *Necronomicon* of mind-blowing paintings derived from his writings, the Sage of Providence would tell you (ever so politely) that you were gibbering mad. If you somehow managed to show him a copy of this book, he would conclude you were Nyarlathotep. In the 1930s, such a volume could have only come from another planet. Verily, the artwork that has grown out of the Lovecraftian tradition is like *nothing* that was available in Lovecraft's time. Compared to Giger or Palencar or Bob Eggleton, the master assassinations of Andrew Brosnatch are exposed as the retarded scrawls that they are. Lovecraft himself would have been amazed, awed, and occasionally revolted by what he saw here. He himself greatly underestimated his own merit and importance; he regarded himself as a failure, like Keats, "a name written on water." But this retrospective proves, if we needed any further proof, that Lovecraft's legacy has instead risen like Great Cthulhu out of the depths, and will continue to go on and on, filling our dreams and turning them into nightmares. ☙

www.ingramcontent.com/pod-product-compliance
Lightning Source LLC
Chambersburg PA
CBHW082050220626
47052CB00006B/1204